THE PEOPLE WHO DRANK WATER FROM THE RIVER

THE PEOPLE WHO DRANK WATER FROM THE RIVER

JAMES KENNEDY

POOLBEG

A Paperback Original
First published 1991 by
Poolbeg Press Ltd
Knocksedan House,
Swords, Co Dublin, Ireland

© James Kennedy, 1991
The moral right of the author has been asserted.

ISBN 1 85371 141 1

Cover illustration and design by Chris Reid
Chapter illustrations by Chris Reid
Set by Richard Parfrey in ITC Stone 10/15
Printed by The Guernsey Press Company Ltd,
Vale, Guernsey, Channel Islands

For Harry, link man between past and present in Brackile,
and for Percy whose soul never left it.

CONTENTS

INTRODUCTION

When I was growing up in East Limerick there were no motor cars passing by our house, no plastic bags, no sellotape, no ballpoint pens, no birthday celebrations, no Mother's Day cards, no Tipp-Ex.

Our money, which came from selling milk to the creamery and calves to West of Ireland calf buyers, was kept under the mattress by my father. There was very little of it to spare for extravagances. Neither was there any ambition to find ways to invest it or multiply it.

As a breed we seemed to lack any aspiration other than to make do and enjoy life. There was no ambition to take over the world and exercise real power. There wasn't an entrepreneur among the lot of us. Neither were there any complaints about deprivation. I never heard any of my uncles or aunts whispering about how to make money or succeed in business. There was never any whispering done except about some girl who got herself into trouble. That is also true of my own brother and sisters. We have been criticised for it by our spouses whom, I suppose, come from more enterprising breeds. They call us lackadaisical, fatalistic.

Lackadaisical we are not. Fatalistic, yes, in a way. Whatever fate dished up was accepted and polished up a bit. Just a bit. Any more would be real enterprise and it might interfere with living just as a motorbike would interfere with a Bushman of the Kalahari. I never had any illusions but that this attitude was a disability as well as a virtue. Because of it I married a woman who was methodical and rigid about

i

things. She is necessary like the men of enterprise onto whose coat tails I now hang for a livelihood.

We have a tendency to work hard at what some people called inconsequential things. Our ten acres were kept drained, the *geosadáns* (ragwort) pulled, the ditches breasted, and a cow never went hungry. The pikes and reeks of hay were neatly trimmed and tied down and our pigs (dead, of course) were cut up with surgical precision. Handles of implements were made and leather, whether it was for horses' tackling or our boots, was sewn and greased. I am proud of these things. Proud enough to record aspects of that lifestyle as a kind of social document so that my children, in later years, will, at least, half know where they come from.

While I'm doing that I've realised that there isn't a generation gap between me and them. There's a two-century gap.

I grew up with the trappings and technology of the nineteenth century in rural Ireland, they with ET of the twenty-first.

CHAPTER 1

Earth

I come from the townland of Brackile in the parish of Grean at the butt-end of East Limerick. The County Tipperary border surrounds our place on two sides, running like the blade of a reaping hook along the hills which stretch from Sologhead at the south, through Carnahalla, Cappawhite, Hollyford, Kilcommon to Rearcross at the north.

I recollect that we crossed the border into Tipperary to go to fairs, to buy bonhams and suits of clothes, to have teeth pulled and, once in a while, to court a Tipperary woman at dusk, down some boreen.

Apart from that we left Tipperary people alone.

Neither did we mingle that much with the real Limerick people who began to take on the real Limerick accent at Dromkeen, three miles on the road to Limerick city and at Herberstown, five miles away on the road to Cork.

The fact that we lived in the old barony of Coonagh which stretched across the border into Tipperary probably accounted for our accent and idioms being more Tipperary than Limerick. I was confirmed in this opinion after reading Kickham's *Knocknagow* for the second time when I was old enough to understand what he was saying. His characters used the same idioms as we did. The first time I read *Knocknagow* I was twelve and didn't notice that because I hadn't learned to be curious about things outside myself.

Our area was a kind of Liechtenstein, of no great social or historical significance to either of the counties surrounding it. Maybe that was the reason we had a reputation for faction fighting at the fairs of the last century and for being rowdy at club hurling matches in Limerick this century. We must have felt we didn't belong to either county and therefore, we had no reputations to keep.

The land around us is flattish with occasional limestone and basalt humps and outcrops. It is drained by two rivers to the north—the Bilbo and the Dead which come together at a lonesome place we called The Joining, two good miles away. The two rivers then become the Mulkear which flows into the Shannon below Annacotty, twenty miles away.

The Joining was a great place for worm-fishing in a flood.

One of the limestone outcrops which later became a quarry was Sarsfield's Rock in Ballyneety, fifteen miles from Limerick city and two miles away from our house as the crow flies. As youngsters we could see it clearly out over the half-door of our thatched house. Sarsfield's Rock was the greatest claim to fame we had. In 1690 Patrick Sarsfield and "Galloping" Hogan rode along the reaping hook from Rearcross to Ballyneety and blew up the Williamite siege-train and its famous big gun the "Sheila Wee" as it was on its way from Waterford to breach the stubborn walls of Limerick.

It was our bad luck again that the history books deprived us of that solitary distinction by accrediting the site to another Ballyneety, only seven miles from Limerick. To be quite honest, of course, our people had nothing to do with blowing up the siege-train. The bang went off at night while they were asleep. But I remember being peeved at the thought of the site being claimed by some other townland.

The only legacy left to us by Sarsfield was the legend that he buried the gold from the siege-train in a field nearby. It was too heavy, people said, to carry on the backs of the tired horses all the way back to Limerick city.

I was once shown the field where it was buried. I was also told that its exact whereabouts could be determined if I watched where snow first melted in the field after a heavy fall. Over a period of years we made a beeline for the field during a thaw but we were always either too early or too late.

The gold is still lying there! None of us, of course, has a spoonful of enterprise where soft money is concerned. We have never thought that money could be got the soft way. Our expectations just wouldn't extend that far.

The name of our barony—Coonagh or *Uí Cuanagh* ("of the soft green land")—was a very poetic perception of our place. The reality was that, as small farmers on land which was damp to soggy, we fought a continuing battle with rushes.

Our family's situation wasn't the worst because our land was on a gentle slope and was well-drained by my father and his forefathers. There was a farm beside us, on the downhill side, which had nothing but rushes—and there's still nothing but rushes on it. Another neighbour below us (who had little but rushes himself) used to call that farm "marmalade." He said it was so soft that if you stood on one side of a field the other side would cock up.

I'm only saying these things to make it clear that the Dead and Bilbo rivers were never any good for drainage. And that's still the way despite all sorts of lobbying to initiate a Mulkear river drainage scheme.

On the other hand, we had great grass in the summertime, a factor which long ago determined that our land was better for grazing cattle than for growing crops. For all practical purposes the only crop cultivation which took place in Brackile was in the haggarts beside the houses, most of which were mud-walled and thatched up to the early 1900s. (Our house is one of the few still surviving.) The haggarts sustained cabbage and potatoes and a few of the lesser vegetables year after year because they were kept nourished by horseloads of cow-dung. Cow-dung was the one agricultural by-product my family never had a shortage of.

In conventional wisdom there has to be someone famous to boast about in a family—a general in the Boer War, a nationalist guerrilla, a missionary bishop in darkest Africa—before one plucks up the courage to write about it. I want to dwell on my family because they were famous for nothing.

This has relevance to other families in the parish of Grean, particularly those who endured on the land on small farms of between ten and fifty acres and who shared with us the same history, geography, and sociology for two hundred years and more. I consider my crowd to be a kind of historical stereotype of the others. This leaves me free to tell what I know about the way we lived without embarrassment because we were all in the same boat.

Admittedly, there was a distinction between the smaller and bigger holdings in Grean. A man who owned the latter was called a "respectable farmer." He was the one who had the bull in the field, the pump in the yard and the son a priest.

We had neither bull nor pump.

When one of our cows demonstrated a need for the bull we children led her by a rope tied to her horns to a neighbour's Hereford bull and watched the copulation process with much the same sangfroid as if both animals had been eating turnips.

When we needed water we went to a stream below the house where there was a flagstone and a shallow pool to dip the bucket in. Our only concession to health and hygiene was the bucket which was white enamelled and which had a special lid for keeping the dust of the kitchen off the water. The buckets for milking were made of galvanised tin.

Years later in the tropics I had reason to be thankful that the river-water had immunised me in my youth. I could drink the tropical water without getting amoebic dysentery. A Clareman who soldiered with me in the same province could do the same—only with more credibility. The water in his bailiwick had been scientifically tested and when the findings came back from the laboratory they read: "Not only is this water unfit for human consumption; it is not even fit for industrial use."

My family did, eventually, rise above itself and had a son a priest for a while in the '60s and '70s but he reverted to type and, of all things, married a brown woman with slanty eyes while he was out trying to convert Southeast Asia. That didn't help to make respectable farmers out of us either.

There are more important implications for my children in my version of our family and its circumstances.

In middle life I came to believe that the mixture of genes of two grandfathers and two grandmothers in all of us constitutes the substance of our identity—who we are, what stuff is in us. Everything else about us develops from there with the help of a few little things like the environment we grow up in, the people we associate with, the education we get and the kind of work we do.

As a result of this new faith I never despaired at the worst of times. I could always glance behind me at uncles and grand-uncles (and at aunts and grand-aunts, of course) and see how many of them stuck to their guns in adversity and were even able to laugh about it. I never gave in, then, to the temptation to hand myself over for support and protection to an ideology but I was content to wander on, sometimes shaking with fear, and guided only by an instinct that human nature—my human nature—was capable of adjusting and renewing itself after any of life's crises.

Fate left my father, Paddy, in Brackile to be the link man

between the past and the present for his generation. In one way it was a prison sentence for him because he had a job in the Garda Síochána for the taking after the Civil War. He chose to stay at home to mind his mother and the bit of land. Perhaps he chose by instinct rather than logically. He was the oldest of the second family of seven of my grandfather James and although he had little love for school he was, for me, more infallible than the Pope while I was growing up.

There was one instance, though, in his life when I saw his confidence crack and the emotional attachment he had for the small farm, which had been handed down to him, revealed. He was about sixty years of age then. I had come home from college for Christmas holidays at age nineteen or twenty years knowing that my only brother who was to carry on my father's work had gone to Manchester the previous October to work in the buildings with a neighbour. Together my father and I let the cows out in the morning and drove them up the hill to the quarry for a drink. He asked me did I think Harry would come back. I could say only that I didn't know. Then, unbelievably, he started to sob and I still remember him saying, "Who will look after the little place when I'm gone?" He went on about his mother and his father and I was so shocked and dumbfounded I didn't hear any more.

Then, as suddenly as the outburst had started, it stopped. "It's a quare world," he said and looked away from me at the sky.

He never mentioned the subject again and my brother did come back—and is still there—the fifth son in a line going back to the 1700s. The roll of the dice of our country's history and economics has made it possible for him to increase our father's acreage fourfold and still remain a small farmer.

I know he has given serious thought to breaking the link with Brackile and moving out to higher ground and a more compact spread. Yet the memory of our ancestors is linked to Brackile, the echo of their footsteps is there. My only real riches is that they stood their ground with wit and without bitterness. They made their implements, drained their fields, grew their crops, tended their animals. They must have seen the irony of it all. If they didn't they would have taken themselves seriously and got out.

In the 1800s they knew that "London was the thinking head" and they "the working hands and feet." There must have been periods of high hope and then bitter disappointment. The hope of the Treaty of Limerick had turned to the humiliation of the Penal Laws. Then more hope after the French Revolution and more defeat after the failed insurrection of 1798. Violence changed to non-violence with Daniel O'Connell driving his parliamentary coach-and-four through the House of Commons, challenging its representatives to change the social, economic and political position of inferiority they had devised for their Gaelic neighbours.

When James Kennedy's tenant farm of twenty-five acres was surveyed in 1834 for tithe-assessment he had two brothers beside him in Brackile—Dan who occupied sixteen acres and Matthew who occupied three. Forty-four acres had been subdivided between them by their father whose name I do not know. James Kennedy was my great-great-grandfather.

He couldn't own the land he occupied. His status as a forty-shilling freeholder disenfranchised him. He paid rent and tithe. The machinery of the state was organised against him. The sheriff was backed up by troops. The magistrate could refuse him justice and not be held accountable. The landlord and the parson oppressed him, not with "beat-him-over-the-head" oppression; but by voting against any change in his favour they kept the deck stacked against him. His Protestant neighbours had the advantage of him at every turn.

So, James of 1834 and, after him, his son William and, after him, his son, James, my grandfather, held their heads down for seventy-five years and kept away from the high ascendancy walls surrounding Linfield House, Sunville, Mount Catherine and Derk. Then at last in 1909 the land could be purchased outright with financing from the state.

Patrick, my father, then inherited it. The only problem was that it had been reduced to ten acres.

William, his grandfather, had occupied ten acres in 1852, according to the records of Griffith's *Land Valuation*.. William's elder brother, John, had twelve acres and another, Daniel, had three, but in partnership with William. So, James's twenty-five acres had again been sub-divided! The three acres which William occupied in partnership with Dan was exchanged for two sacks of yellow corn during the Famine. There was an arrangement that the use of it would again revert to William in better times. That never happened and it led to bitterness between our family and that of the user and new owner which lasted down to my day.

William needed the sacks of corn because he had nine children to feed. The eldest, Mary, was born on 9 April 1841 and died at eight or nine. My grandfather James, William's oldest son, was born after Mary on 29 March 1842. He went blind in his fifties and had to have the *Freeman's Journal* read to him. He lived to be eighty. Two of his four brothers— Dan, a cooper, and Patrick (supposed to have been the most handsome man in the parish)—emigrated to America. They were either part of the forty-two percent of the population of Limerick which emigrated between 1851 and 1871 or they went shortly afterwards. Nobody ever heard from them again. The rest of the brothers and sisters found places for themselves through marriage in Limerick and Tipperary. Some of their descendants have kept in touch. Others we have lost track of.

William lived on to become the first chairman (then called captain) of the Gaelic Athletic Association in Grean in 1887 and he used to walk the mile and a half to eleven o'clock Mass in Nicker every Sunday to lead the prayers before Mass. Bridgie Gleeson, a next-door neighbour who died in 1963 at the age of eighty-seven, told me that. She had never been out of the parish in her life but she could walk the legs off a cock-pheasant and had a memory like a computer.

That leaves only my father's generation to account for. They were the second family to be provided for out of ten acres and they were nine too. Grandfather James had two children by a first marriage to a local woman, Johanna Creed, who died in 1891 when they were small. They were Bill and Nonie. Both of them stayed in the parish until they died. Nonie married a quarryman from Nicker and had nine children, most of whom are in America or England now. She was droll and unpretentious and came back to our place often, particularly to have "her hooves pared" as she called it by father. She also cut the *scilleáns* for us in springtime.

Bill became the local schoolmaster and taught all of us— even his younger half-brother Mike and half-sister Missie. He also taught the girl who became his wife. I will have more to say about him.

My father had four brothers following him in the second family, Simon, Jack, Jim, Mike, and two sisters, Maria and Julie who was known as "Missie." Simon and Jack went to America, Mike married a local woman with a pub but moved to Dublin, and the two sisters Maria and Missie left the parish too, and married respectively a small farmer and a garda. Jim, my godfather, became the local creamery manager. He played solo with the parish priest and was giving a pound to the church collection when my father was only giving three shillings and sixpence. I inherited his love of books and he was the first person to explain sex for people as distinct from sex for animals to me.

These are my crowd. Their genes and much of their emotional and rational reflexes crisscrossed me and my generation. I feel that many of the crises, decisions and searchings in my life, have all happened before—through them. When my time came to leave the parish at eighteen I was only obeying history or repeating it. I was the oldest, had little interest in cows and dung and had a leaving cert from the CBS in Doon. That was as much, if not more than the ten acres could afford me. I then went on a wild-goose chase. Some of it took me around the world. After twenty-five years I came back because the memories of Brackile would not go away.

CHAPTER 2

Fire

The open fire in our kitchen had a chimney so wide it had to be cleaned by pulling a furze bush downwards through it with a rope.

It had an iron crane, on which hung a four-gallon metal pot, a bastable for baking bread and a big metal kettle. The crane, about chest high, had two adjustable (up and down) pot hooks. It could also swing out on its axis from the hob in case a pot, boiling over, had to be removed quickly from above the flames.

There was a blower in the corner to fan the flames to life. It had a wooden handle, shiny with age, with which to twist its big wheel round and round. By my time that wood (probably ash) was worn down almost to the axle by the right hands of four generations of mothers and children. When strangers came, few of them knew what function the blower had and they and their children would be particularly excited at seeing the flames rise when we let them twist the wheel.

Our fire was the only source of heat in the house which was warm because it was thatched to twelve inches in thickness and had mud walls. I never remember being cold there even though you could look up the wide chimney on a frosty night and see the stars.

My mother did all the baking and cooking on the open fire. Not only did she cook for the family, she also had to boil pots of yellow meal and potatoes for the pigs and hens. In bad weather she dried the washing—draped over the back of our *súgán* chairs—in front of it. The hob which blackened quickly with the smoke and rivulets of sooty rain had to be whitewashed regularly with a mixture of lime and water, especially when visitors were coming.

The fire was the centre of life for us for six months of the year—October to March—when darkness came early and the weather was cold. We sat round the hearth when the oil lamp was lit. We did our homework, read, played cards or draughts. Mother sewed, darned, baked a late cake or read Annie MP Smithson. My father went out a lot on his bicycle but when he was there he rarely read. He initiated quizzes for us and in the end I think we knew everything about geography, anatomy, trees, insects and so on that he knew. He had left school in fourth class, but had a wide knowledge of the world and of natural history.

Encouraged to be curious about the world and its people we picked up much of our general knowledge when neighbours dropped in for *cuartaíocht* and we listened to the conversations. One night, as we sat around, the soot kept falling from the chimney and we knew that rain was coming. This led to a conversation about the weather and how the new moon related to it. My younger sister, Mary, interrupted.

"What do they do with the old moons, Daddy?"

Billy Gleeson, our nearest neighbour, shot back, "They make stars out of them, alanna."

It was here more than anywhere else my brother and sisters and I learned to be unafraid of people and the relationships we create with them through words and gestures and feelings. If there was one thing I learned then which was very helpful to me later in life it was the ability to join in discussions without fear or difficulty. There were no barriers built up in us around the fire. There was respect for the other man or woman, farm-worker, servant-girl or the well-to-do, and a genuine curiosity about their respective stories.

We kept our fire going with timber and turf. The timber was oak, ash, elm, sycamore, blackthorn and whitethorn. We used only the trimmed branches of trees, rarely the trees themselves which we treasured in much the same way we treasured our animals. The whitethorn called the *sgeach* was the most common species. Since it was more of a bush than a tree and thorny to boot, it was widely used on ditches as fencing. Its thorns caused many a septic finger and foot in rural Ireland.

My father had a wooden block at the back of the house on which he chopped kindling and sawed blocks for the fire. He had an extravagant way of putting kindling on the open fire—with a pitchfork. This used to infuriate my mother who wanted her fire always to be tidy. I remember arguments flying about whose fire it was anyway and the utter consternation of my mother, when, once in a while, my father would pee on the fire to quench it before going to bed on a cold night. (We had no indoor toilet.) Logs would sizzle and clouds of ash would drift up on the crane. The fire had to be quenched every night in a thatched house, according to him, and one kind of water was as good as another to do it with.

Years later I was reminded of this when somebody told me about Peggy Guggenheim and Jackson Pollock. Peggy Guggenheim (of the Guggenheim Museum in New York) became a famous patroness of the arts and used to invite young artists to her Park Avenue home for dinner of an evening. She admitted that she was never sure of the talent of Jackson Pollock until one evening, in the middle of mixed company, he sauntered over to her enormous fireplace in the drawing room and, unabashed, peed into it. Peggy was terribly impressed and Jackson Pollock did go on to become one of the greatest of modern American artists.

My mother was no Peggy Guggenheim.

We bought turf by the lorry-load from Claremen after a lot of arguing about the price. They came round during early autumn. We didn't cut turf ourselves because the nearest bog producing good turf was at Comer in the mountains near Rearcross. This was ten miles away. We didn't have the time in summer to save our hay and turf as well.

When the war came the turfmen from Clare deserted us because they got a better price from industry. We were then forced to take to the bog ourselves and work at a job we were quite unfamiliar with.

I remember a week in early summer of 1941, or '42 when we were supposed to set out for the bog but my father got the flu. He was isolated in the press bed in the parlour because my mother didn't want his many visitors sizing up our bedroom. Since the flu prevented him from going on his bicycle to listen to "Lord Haw-Haw" at night on a neighbour's radio (we didn't have one) he sent me to the village of Pallas to get the *Irish Independent*. Sick and all as he was, he wanted to keep up with the progress of the war.

When I came back he looked up at me with a drawn, fluey face, made greyer by a week's growth of stubble.

"Read me out the headings," he commanded.

"Germans Fall Back," I announced.

"Oh, shit!" he said.

We went to the bog shortly after that, he on his bicycle and me on the bar. The *sleán* (the implement, like a spade, used for cutting turf) with its cutting edges wrapped in a piece of sacking was strapped to the bar under me. He had borrowed it from mother's sister and her husband in Foilacleara who had their own bog on the top of Knocnastanna. Strapped to the carrier of the bike was a basket carrying tea and sugar, buttered bread, a billy-can and two tin canisters to drink from. I had never been in a bog before and, at the age of eight, couldn't wait to paddle around in my bare feet in its black ooze, to make a fire and drink tea out of a tin canister.

The bog we went to, however, wasn't Comer but Castlegarde, only four miles away. It was a flat bog of mediocre, quick-burning turf, which had just been opened to the public by its owner to cope with the fuel emergency. It was overgrown with birches and we spent as much time digging out roots as we did cutting and "footing."

We were an ill-assorted group—shopkeepers, gardaí, small farmers—and the camaraderie that existed was born out of the uncertainty and novelty of the job before us.

When the turf was drying in small stacks before being put into one big stack to be measured, paid for and taken home, a garda who was the Superintendent's clerk in Pallas kept saying his stacks were getting smaller. There was a lot of whispering among the men and I suspected they were making plans to catch a turf-thief who obviously came at night.

A few days passed.

Then one lunchtime when all of us were tending to our own fires and billy-cans there was an explosion at the Super's clerk's fire. I had a glimpse of sparks, sods of turf and his billy-can going up in the air. Suddenly there was laughter from all around when it dawned on everyone what had happened: the garda's scheme of putting a small quantity of gunpowder into selected sods for the thief had misfired. Unwittingly, he had burned one of the sods of turf that he had "mined" for the enemy.

When the turf was dry we borrowed a donkey from Uncle Bill to haul it out to the road on a sheet of galvanised iron.

The donkey was lighter than our three-quarter horse which my father couldn't risk on the spongy surface of the bog. I used to ride the donkey bareback the three miles to the bog and back while my father brought horse and wagon. Between us we brought the turf home.

That was the only time we ever went to the bog, and, in the end, I wasn't unhappy about that. The bareback donkey riding gave me the most painful boil in the ass I ever had. I had to go to bed and have it lanced by the doctor. The summer experience of the bog which began for us in the press bed also ended up there.

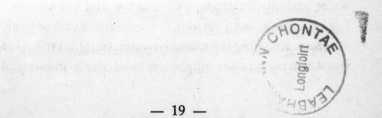

CHAPTER 3

Play

I walked the bank of the river that twisted its way by the water meadow and kept glancing into the pools where the trout lay. I came to my favourite spot. A black sally hung over a bend where the water was two feet deep. When I waved my arms the trout took off and darted under the hairy roots of the black sally, leaving faint trails of muddy water behind. I went upstream, stripped to my shirt (we never wore underpants then) and muddied the water with my feet so that the trout would not see me. I began groping, foot after foot, downstream under the bank, my fringe touching the muddied water. I felt four fish. One was worth taking and I cupped one hand over its mouth and gills and the other around its tail. It floated gently and unafraid against my fingers. A gentle squeeze and I'd got my supper.

Had I a diary for the summers of 1948-52 I could have written this regularly. In later years my brother and I became fly-fishing addicts but walking the bed of the river in our bare feet was enough then.

That and the swimming hole which we made by damming the cold water of our little river which had no name. Cows sheltered from the July sun upstream under the railway bridge. When we swam in the early afternoon, rather than with the men, after milking time, the water was sometimes yellowish with cow-shit and urine.

My sisters Breda and Mary and their friend Josie Byrane got us to make a smaller dam for them a few hundred yards downstream. It was not that they were fastidious about bathing in the "Yellow River"; it was just that they felt that our swimming hole, at three feet, was too deep for them.

Harry and I worked for a few hours and completed a dam with rocks, mud and *feileastraim* (yellow flags) until the water was about a foot and a half deep. Come afternoon the three girls appeared, wearing white vests which my mother had stitched at the crotch to make one-piece swim-suits. They giggled and shivered and oohed and aahed but refused to put a foot in the eighteen inches of water. They settled for the downriver side of the dam where there was an inch of water, small rocks and skeins of green scummy moss. There, crouched down and with sharp intakes of breath and squeals, they were happy that, at long last, they were swimming.

But fishing and swimming and hunting played second fiddle to the great passion of our lives—hurling. It ran in the family. Half the Pallas hurling team sometime previously was made up of the Ryans of Cross (who lived less than a quarter-mile away) and my father and his brothers. There were so many broken hurleys about the place that many of our tools, such as hammers and hatchets, had the end of a hurley as a handle. I never used a bought hurley. My father made them all and gave me my first one when I was about six.

It became my constant companion like the assegai of a young Masai. I learned to wield it against daisies and piss-a-beds. I drove the cows with it. It served as a Sharps rifle in cowboys and indians. Few days passed without a puck-around in the paddock or on the road in front of the house. We would be sent to pull *geosadáns* and the hurleys would be hidden so that when my father went in we would puck around again.

The time came for my first competitive hurling match. It was for Doon CBS (called St Fintan's) against Cashel and I was fifteen. All the years of pucking around in the paddock and on the road would be tested. My mother sewed up a pair of knicks for me out of a flour bag. I think the ANK of RANKS FLOUR was up near the elastic and I could cover it with the appalling white-brown jersey of St Fintan's. I played left full back. My opponent got two goals off me. I never forgot that. It was a great humiliation. My father had held the great Tipperary full forward, Hughie Shelly, scoreless in the few matches they played against one another.

There was plenty of time for all sorts of other play in

Brackile. I think my parents were wise in encouraging us to do so because many of our contemporaries were inducted into farming responsibilities at too early an age and missed out on may of the hectic hours and adventures which we enjoyed, running wild.

We lived on a quarter-mile straight, two thirds of the way up a steep hill. We built go-cars, tricycles, toboggans to take advantage of the gradient. These were our toys. We were good at hammering, sawing, chiselling, clinching, boring because we saw our father at it. He allowed us his tools (all but his wood chisels) but never helped us make anything, nor praised our workmanship. It seems to me now that it was believed that the greatest disaster that could befall an Irish father's son was that he might get a swelled head from a modicum of affirmation.

They tell the story of a middle-aged man and a youth in his early twenties sitting at a bar. The man was laying into the younger over something and a stranger who was drinking by himself intervened:

"Why are you insulting that young man?" he asked.

"What's wrong with insulting him?" the elder responded. "He's my son."

My father certainly observed the custom that you should not be seen to praise your own child. If we played well in a hurling or football match he'd say nothing. If we made mistakes, he'd pounce on us.

One day during a football match in Caherconlish I got a kick in the ribs when I tried to block down a ball being kicked by Timmy Reardon of Knockane. When I got up I couldn't breathe properly and, in distress, I headed for the sideline. My father shouted:

"Where are you going?"

"There's something wrong with me," I answered. "I can't breathe."

"There's nothing wrong with you. Get back in there, again!"

I turned around and went back in and at the first tackle fell down again and had to come off.

I had three broken ribs, not cracked or fractured, but broken.

I took it as perfectly normal that you didn't give up anything until you were incapable of going on. It wasn't a bad principle, and in my life, I've never regretted it nor blamed my father for being a hard taskmaster. Anyway, there was another side to him. He was the one who, very gently, took thorns out of our feet in summer, checked that we always had dry feet in wet conditions. (He mended our boots and shoes on the days on which it would be too wet to work outside.) He responded immediately with cuts of bread and jam if any of us were hungry and went to great lengths to warn us of all the dangers (from poisonous berries to sharp instruments) that were inherent in rural life.

There was a day, though, when his no-praise syndrome misfired. For five minutes at half time in a football semi-final against Claughaun, in Hospital, I and, in particular, my brother, were affirmed and supported publicly by him and Uncle Jim. And the shock of it, for both of us, led to great melodrama.

I was playing in goal and Harry, aged seventeen, was getting his first outing in the senior team as a corner forward. I believe the coach intended giving Harry a run in the first half and replacing him by another youngster at half time. But Harry threw a spanner in the works by playing well, scoring a goal and a few points, and laying on more.

My father and uncle Jamesey, as usual, stood out on the fringe of the crowd on the sideline. They were big men and wore wide, soft hats. I was saying to myself this looks like being one of the days we'll get no criticism from Pop. (We called my father Pop in his latter years.)

At half time the two of them sauntered on to the pitch where our team were standing or lying on the ground, talking among themselves and to supporters and well-wishers. Some of us took a few drags of a cigarette. One or two I knew had a slug out of a baby Power. We were all in high spirits at having secured a very surprising lead over Claughaun.

Then Harry was told by the coach that he was being replaced and he accepted it without murmur. When he announced this to Pop and Jamesey, their faces got red and Harry couldn't believe it when he heard them saying:

"But that's ridiculous. You're playing well. Why should you go off?"

He was being praised!

"Because so-and-so said so," answered Harry.

"What does he know about football!" said the two.

Suddenly it flashed to Harry that he was now the victim of a bad decision and he got red-faced too. When the Kennedys get heated up they do so with the speed of lightning!

Next thing there were "words" between Harry and the

coach. A fracas developed and restraining hands and words had to be laid on both. In high dudgeon Pop stalked off to the sideline, Harry with him. I had never seen him so angry.

He had wanted me to abandon the game with Harry but I wouldn't. I couldn't. But I did make some verbal contribution during the melodrama—and in very unclerical language.

We won.

I was reported to Dalgan Park by the curate for using the word "shit." I was nearly expelled. Harry got the worst of it. The club suspended him for a year.

When I think of it now it was Pop and Jamesey who should have been suspended. To support and affirm us out of the blue like that was just too much!

CHAPTER 4
Clay

Invariably, a day would come each winter when my father would stand in the middle of the kitchen floor and announce, "There's a rat in the pit!"

These lines were as carefully chosen by him for his audience as Shakespeare chose Portia's "This bond doth give thee here no jot of blood..." which turned the tables on Shylock in *The Merchant of Venice*.

Even our terrier, Buddy, seemed to know something was up: that the pit of potatoes would be probed gradually, perhaps stripped, until the rat made a run for it and he would die like the thief he was.

When our Kerr's Pinks were dug out in the autumn they

were housed in what we called a pit. The word pit gives the wrong impression—that of a hole into which potatoes were thrown. In reality the pit was an above ground earthen cladding which covered the mound of potatoes and kept them dry and cut off from the light during the winter and spring. It was covered also with straw and one end was kept open so that we could get at our daily supply for domestic use.

For a rambling rat the pit became an apartment-cum-restaurant at our expense.

In our minds as children the thought of the hunt and then the revenge on this rodent generated out-of-the-ordinary excitement and mercilessness.

I clearly remember the first of many of these rat-hunts.

The four of us, two boys and two girls aged four to ten (a third sister was by this time living with an aunt and her husband who had no children of their own), stood at the ready around the pit with hurleys, while my father carefully probed it with the blunted tooth of a "getherer." My mother held the dog who quivered and slavered from instinct because rat-catching was in his breed.

"Watch out now," my father roared. "I'm coming near the end. If he's there he'll come out the hole."

We stiffened in apprehension.

Then the rat made a run for it, a grey streak shooting across ten yards of space to an old stone wall. Hurleys swung. The dog snarled and leaped. My father bellowed, "There he is. Get him."

The dog hit my small sister and knocked her over. The rat shot through my brother's legs. I swung the hurley and hit my brother on the shins. When I turned round to follow the flight of the rat I got a wallop in the backside from my brother in retaliation. The rat escaped. My mother laughed.

"Mother of Jaysus," my father exclaimed shaking his head, "Me and my staff!"

That was the only rat I ever remember escaping. The following years our defences were better and, like the Mounties, we always got our man.

But the pit is a long way from the spring day when Auntie Nonie would come to cut the *scilleáns*. Why she was the one to cut up the seed potatoes so that there was a bud or an eye on each piece, I don't know. My father certainly thought of her as an expert at it. Nowadays farmers use whole potatoes as seed but that's because they're usually planted in drills, opened and closed by a plough.

A *bán* (bawn), a fresh field turned into garden by upturning the sods into ridges with a spade, was a different kettle of fish. If the seed potatoes were too big they wouldn't fit into the small hole made by the spade on the ridges. I remember the *scilleáns* being sprinkled with lime to keep the slugs off and then kept in sacks until the days for sowing came around.

The first to be tilled was the haggart. My father, with a cloth patch safety-pinned on his left knee to keep his britches from wearing, would have the haggart dug early and a few drills of early potatoes sown as well as lines of common and York cabbage.

Once that was out of the way he concentrated on the quarter or half quarter acre of *bán* we would lease with others from some big farmer with good land in the area. We were on the fringe of the Golden Vale—on the damp side of it. Good land rose with the higher ground to the southwest of us.

There was no need of my presence while the digging of the *bán* was in progress. It was all done with a spade and it was men's work. I came on the scene when the ridges were made. They were three-sod ridges, roughly eighteen inches wide, that were always as straight as a die. I never saw a string-line used and, to this day, don't know how they did it.

Then my father put on the *máilín*, filled it up with *scilleáns* and started to dig them in. It was great to watch. Thump the spade went into the ridge, driven deep by my father's hob-nailed boot on the tilly. A push forward on the handle and a hole appears behind the blade, Plonk, a *scilleán* from the *máilín* is tossed unerringly into the hole. My job is to follow him and thump the hole closed with a pounder which looks like a polo-stick. Some men could sow potatoes faster than a machine nowadays. The secret lay in being able to keep a fist of *scilleáns* in the hand while digging and drop them accurately into the hole.

The garden, like the bog, had a lot of phases to it, a lot of back-breaking work and a social life all of its own which was often entertaining.

My father had taught Joe Ryan how to throw a spud over a hundred yards by impaling it on a pointed stick about four or five feet long and whipping it into the air. A neighbour was working away at his own plot less than a hundred yards away when spuds began to lob into the stalks beside him. He couldn't figure out where the spuds were coming from since no one was within normal throwing distance of him. He'd look up and down and walk around and go back to his spade. When he started digging Joe would lob another one and keep his head down as if he was working away. And so it went on.

"It must be the crows," the victim said to my father afterwards. "Although when I looked up at the sky there were no crows. It's a bit of a mystery," he concluded as if he was coming across mysteries every second day.

I heard my father talk about the caffling that went on when many of the Brackile people had a garden in Bobby Ryan's of Newtown. They were trenching the ridges one day—setting back through the young stalks while shovelling clay from the furrow up around them. When Malachy Ryan went away to make the tea they prawbed the handle of his shovel with dung. And if that wasn't enough they dug a hole a few yards back the furrow and concealed it with stalks. Malachy, naturally, was furious when he smelled his hands after the first shovelful but he got in a real rage and went after Joe Ryan (who laughed loudest but wasn't guilty) with the shovel when he picked himself out of the hole in the furrow, five minutes later.

If digging *bán* with a spade, sowing and trenching had become an art-form when I witnessed it in the early 1940s, it must have been quite a sight one hundred years earlier when there was four times the population to be dug and trenched for. I have seen the faint outline of old ridges in the most unarable fields around us in Brackile—testimony to the need for ground to grow a good spud on. When considering the potato crop which failed in 1846 and 1847 nobody has ever mentioned the dogs, the pigs and the hens which were fed with potatoes, too. Did they sicken and die like the humans? In our own day I know that the dog was the best fed of all of us. He got the skins of the spuds and the cabbage water. Dieticians tell us now that the best part of the potato is the skin and since Irish housewifes usually boiled the devil out of the cabbage much of its vitamins remained in the water.

I'm quite sure that many of the rural Irish of my generation who emigrated found it hard to get the appetite for spuds, bacon and cabbage out of their systems—even though it was most unlikely to turn up in menus of Kenya, Korea or Katmandu. I know from chastening experience that a midday meal of potatoes is not on in the tropics. They are too heavy on the digestive system, unlike rice which is the staple diet of three-quarters of the world's population.

It came home to me one night in Saigon in 1975 how marginalised the potato had become to my life after four years in Asia. I had a dinner of pigeon, rice and potato. The potato was served as a vegetable with the rice and I couldn't help thinking how the Brackile people would have viewed this. The spuds would have been served as spuds; the rice would come as a pudding with milk and sugar; the pigeons would have been shot for eating the cabbage and left to rot as they fell.

When I returned to Ireland in 1977 and settled down to being a provider for the first time in my life I attempted to do some of the things my father did when he was a provider for us. I was groping around somewhere between the self-sufficient society of the '40s and the consumer society of today. To be quite honest, I didn't know my ass from my elbow but it seemed so simple to grow potatoes for a start.

I rented a plot from Dublin Corporation and made an agreement with my friend Jack Hynes that we would go halves in the work and in the produce. Jack, as it turned out, was a bad influence on me but he did have the right rural, spud-digging pedigree from Cappatagle in County Galway.

The two of us surveyed our one-tenth of an acre allotment proudly in April. Withered hay was growing two feet high in places. We decided to burn the hay and dig the plots with spades just like our fathers did. Digging would be good for us—a sort of jogging for the profit. Then we went for a pint.

When the burning was done we returned for the first dig, spades on shoulders. At the end of two hours we had a patch dug the size of two graves. It didn't remotely resemble the beginnings of a garden. It just looked as if a couple of sows had been rooting there. The digging out of the scutch was what slowed us down and it had given us an awful thirst.

So we went for a pint.

The problem, we agreed, was the "scutch" grass which after I had gone through the S section of various dictionaries turned out to be "couch" grass. When *Chambers* defined it as "a troublesome weed grass owing to its creeping rootstocks," it was quite obvious that the compiler never confronted it in a corporation plot. Its scientific name was *agropyron cristatum* and we wondered (having grown up with Latin) if *cristatum* shouldn't have been *tristatum*. It grew in a solid mat five or six inches thick under the surface and would take a year to dig out. We would have to plough it.

It was ploughed by a tractor for £10 and so deep that we

were confused by the next step. The sods were huge and craggy.

The Sligoman across from us said, "Harrow it, but where you'll get a power harrow, I don't know."

The Corkman, two plots east of us, said, "Do what you like, but don't rotovate it. That will merely spread the scutch."

The Kerryman who always stopped to talk, declared: "It's hard to know what's best."

We kicked sods around, prodded them with spades, and went off for a pint. The problem would have to be worked out in quiet.

We were the only newcomers at our end of the allotment area. We had leased solid scutch, so to speak, because our plots hadn't been tilled in years. Round-Up is an expensive chemical which people said would kill the weed but the process would take a month and it was already May. Anyway, Jack who attended anti-nuclear rallies and protests outside the US embassy convinced me we should be anti-chemical so we found ourselves in a position in which, paraphrasing St. Paul, we could say, "to dig, we are not able, and to spray Round-Up, we are ashamed."

Our unity began to disintegrate then because we couldn't agree on anything save that the ploughed earth should be stirred somehow. Communal thinking and communal action had consistently got us nowhere but to Kenny's pub in Lucan.

I let Jack go his own way and, with a lot of grunting and puffing, I coaxed every two lines of upturned sod into a sort of drill, leaving the matted scutch untouched at the bottom.

I dug in the seed-potatoes every eighteen inches or so, each one lovingly cushioned on a fistful of hops and sprinkled with 10-10-20. If I'd had holy water I'd have sprinkled it on, too.

The stalks came up and so did the scutch. I had the family out grappling with it while I made desperate attempts at trenching or moulding with a shovel. I sprayed twice and spent much of my spare time in July and August on my knees trying to keep the scutch at bay—or at least from dwarfing the stalks. It seemed to grow as fast as I pulled it.

Harvest time came at the end of August and the first Records were a joy on our table. I stuffed myself so that not even a single small one would go to the dog. They were, after all, the first spuds I ever grew. The spud-growing link between the Kennedy generations was being preserved, unbroken.

Then one mid-October evening when I got home from work there was a letter for me from the Corporation.

Brutally, it said: "Dear Mr K, I refer to your letting of allotment No X. Although you have paid for this plot for the 1980 season, it seems that it has not been worked. I should be obliged if you would let me know if you intend to work this plot for the coming season. As there are a number of people on the waiting-list I will have to allocate this plot to one of these unless I hear from you by return. Yours, etc., etc."

I swore by the *máilíns* and *scilleáns* of my ancestors. It was evident that some agent of the Corporation had inspected my plot (most likely from the ditch of the road in case he'd get muck on his shoes) and couldn't distinguish between stalks and scutch in the distance.

To add the final nail in my coffin my wife, who had seen potatoes at 95p a sack in the local supermarket (it was the year of a glut), began totting up what I had spent on allotment fees, seed potatoes, ploughing, hops, fertiliser, petrol, and a new handle for the spade.

"Well?" I asked after the calculations were finished.

"Yours cost us £3.80 a sack, not counting labour," she replied.

"A trifle expensive," I suggested, knowing in my heart that if she added the price of the drink they would be very expensive potatoes, indeed.

Some of us, really, are not a patch on our fathers.

CHAPTER 5

Love

A story is told about a middle-aged bachelor farm-labourer who fell off a roof he was thatching in Plaukerauka in our parish sometime in the 1930s. When the nurse in Barrington's Hospital asked him how the accident happened he had to go back to the year 1900 to begin his story. He walked from North Kerry then, he said, as a spalpeen for the digging of the spuds in Limerick and, on a cold night, ended up in a house in Kildimo where he was taken on for a few days.

When he was going to bed in the loft the only daughter of the house climbed up the ladder and put her head in the small door. In a husky voice she asked, "Are you all right,

Brendan? Can I do anything for you?"

"Oh, I'm great," he replied, "my belly is full and there's a pleasant tiredness on me from all the walking. Thanks very much!"

Next night when the old folks were gone to bed she did the same again only this time she added, "Are you sure you're all right? Can I do anything for you?"

He protested that he couldn't have been better treated, said goodnight and blew out the candle.

The third night she came into the room, sat on the edge of the bed, held his hand and with great concern whispered, "Are you all right, Brendan? Do you really want me to do anything for you?"

"Of course, I'm all right," he insisted. "That rhubarb cake you made today was as good as my mother ever made. I'll miss ye when I go tomorrow."

At this stage the nurse in Barrington's intervened. "What the hell has this story of thirty years ago to do with your breaking your leg?" she asked.

"When I was above in the roof yesterday," he explained, "it dawned on me what the Kildimo woman was up to and with the shock of it I slithered down and fell off."

My love life from the age of four to eighteen was something like Brendan's. Things never dawned on me until the opportunities had passed.

I lived in some sort of never-never land. Whatever romance was in me, fuelled by books like *The Blue Lagoon*, *Coral Island*, those of Maurice Walsh and Zane Grey, stayed in the realm of fantasy. Anytime it came out it was as horseplay or else I backed away from it with the alacrity of a cut cat.

There was a period during secondary school—around the age of sixteen—when women became the rage for many of us. The cinema in the village of Doon became the rendezvous place. It was only a short distance from the Christian Brothers where I went to school and the Mercy convent down the road. Since I lived five miles away and was only allowed to go to the pictures the odd time I had to listen to my contemporaries in the village of Doon talk about sessions with convent girls, some of whom were boarders who would slip over the wall at night. It was mouth-watering, he-man stuff.

Eventually my great moment arrived. After the pictures, one night, the hard men from the village were pairing off with girls and disappearing into the moonlight. I was left with this girl from the mountains who was very pretty.

"Will you go with me?" says I.

"I will," says she.

"Get up on the carrier so," says I.

It was a time for quick breathing. I raced down the Togher road with her on the carrier in case I'd lose any of the occasion's momentum.

I turned in the narrow boreen towards Kilmoylan bog, threw the bicycle up against the ditch and then...I didn't know what to do.

It was a regular feature of country life for courting couples to find a "nest" free of briars in a ditch and lie up against it in one another's arms. I had seen them many times. One night I even greeted a couple in Croughmorca who were locked into one another with a "God bless the work."

The girl from the mountains went over to the ditch and lay up against it. So did I. I didn't touch her.

"I wonder where the others are gone?" I asked.

"I don't know," she replied. "I don't really care."

I was losing my grip. This wasn't a scene from Maurice Walsh. The momentum was going. The spell was breaking. She was just a girl lying against a wet ditch.

We exchanged a few more inconsequential remarks and I said we'd better go back to the village to meet the others.

"Okay," she said.

It was clear after that there was a gap to be bridged by me between women as objects of fantasy to be dreamed about and women as sex objects to be touched and cuddled. My time hadn't come.

But the time had come for the greatest tongue-lashing I ever got—first, as one of a group of "schoolboy womanisers" from Father Lee, the curate in Doon, and secondly, man to man, from Brother Condon, the superior of the school. Some girl had got pregnant, there was a flap on in the convent and the heavies were called in.

Lee's anger (stage-managed, I realise now, because he knew the inside story) lit the place for twenty minutes and we slunk away, terrified. The meeting with Brother Condon whom I liked and who liked me, was unexpected. It took place for effect in the parlour of the Brother's house not in the school.

"I hear you're fond of the women, Kindy," was his opening shot. He called me "Kindy" when he was mad at me.

I didn't know what to say. But he got to me when he said, "What would your mother say if she could see the way you're letting the family down?"

He went on about my mother, knowing it was an Achilles' heel for most young lads and the knife went in deeper and deeper. I could have taken a hammering with the strap but that would have been too easy.

I think he saw me crumbling and, letting me go, added that he had to do this because some of the nuns thought we were all rapists up here.

"Are you, Kindy?" he asked with a sudden smile.

"Not any more, sir," I replied.

From then on I went home another road from school.

The whole business of love and courtship was never talked about at home which was a great pity. I never understood, and still don't, what there is in it to be secretive about. Perhaps it was because of its association with the sexual side of it—the part to do with the sixth and ninth commandments. My mother never mentioned what she thought about love, sex and marriage to me. Once in a while she would join the others in baiting me about Kitty McGrath, a neighbour, and Maidie Franklin, a classmate. I was "in love" with both of them for years but never told anyone, least of all the girls themselves. There seemed to have been a conspiracy to keep the strongest impulses of adolescence in fantasyland.

I have no idea whether that was widespread but I do know that, later on in life, other forces were at work to impede the natural instinct of healthy, well-adjusted men and women to mate. It wasn't the Church which one could always side-step by admitting a liaison in confession. It was the class structure.

I knew of women in the parish—fine women whom any man could be proud of—who never married because the only marital options open to them were to men who might have a farm thirty acres less than their own. The number of eligible single men with land and livelihood, even now, is incredible. The class-social pressure to marry your own kind is almost gone but a different kind of obstacle has cropped up; women don't want to be involved in farming any more.

My mother was a *bean a' tí*. This does not mean that she was a housewife in the modern sense. *Bean a' tí* means *the* woman of *the* house, a title which has some respect built into it. When she left her own six-room, slate house in Coolnamona, Doon to live in the thatched, three-room house in Brackile with my father she brought her *lares* and *penates* with her. (In Roman times these were household gods which families, moving to another location, always took with them.) My mother's *lares* and *penates* were a new picture of the Sacred Heart (signed by her own brother, Jim Lande, a priest in Diamond Creek in the diocese of Melbourne), a tea-set, dinner-set and linen table-cloth, framed pictures of members of her family, dining-room chairs, an embroidered fire screen, ewer and jug, matching vases for the mantelpiece and oil paintings which she completed during her schooldays in Cross and Passion Convent, Kilcullen and Mercy Convent, Doon.

They were displayed in the parlour, one of our three rooms which, for all intents and purposes, became her museum. Although there wasn't a room to spare in our house it was implicit in the marriage contract that she would have this room for her "icons", for the things which emphasised her identity as Nora Lande and which she could show to her friends, proving that her marriage wasn't a takeover but a coming together.

Like all the other farmers' wives that I knew well in Brackile, Kilduff and Tullabeg she worked as a partner with my father and as a partner with us, her children, in the family business of husbanding animals and land.

Her day began at six—in spring, summer and autumn. She lit the fire, hand-milked half of our cows with my father, made breakfast, and got us off to school. From May to November there were pigs to be fed, in the spring, calves and hens all year round. The washing was done by hand in the tin bath-pan with rainwater from the barrel at the end of the house. She used a scrubbing board and thick blocks of Lifebuoy soap. She met us with a smile after school and had our meal ready. Then it was cow-time again and after that, supper. The cake that wasn't baked during the day was baked then. Socks were darned. The sewing machine would whirr as clothes were altered and patches put on.

As I lay in bed I would hear her moving in the kitchen. Once in a while she would sing to herself. She always sang at the cows—"The Old Bog Road." She had a good voice. Then I would hear my father's footsteps coming down the hill in his hobnail boots and turning the corner into the dairy to put in his bike. They would talk. He would give her all the news—slowly. She was never much for going out.

It was a great feeling to be in a feather bed, under a thatched roof, and to know your parents were at ease with one another.

One day when she was eighty-five, she felt she was going to die. She called in my brother, the one of us who lived with her at the time.

"You know I have nothing to leave ye," she said, "but tell the rest of them there's one thing I want from you all. Ye must never fall out with one another."

She lived for another three years and was taken care of by my sister and her husband. Then the life faded slowly away from her and she died with a son and a daughter by her bedside.

My mother taught us about love.

CHAPTER 6

Sweat

When I think back to the period in summer we called "the hay" I have no difficulty in recalling it in vivid detail. I'm sure that it is because I disliked it with an intensity I've never encountered in myself for anything else—animal, vegetable, or mineral.

I shiver when I recall the despondency I felt, at twelve, looking down the length of a swath (mispronounced "swart" by all of us for some reason) of drying hay maybe two hundred yards long which had to be turned with a fork and in tune with three or four grown men who could go left-hand underneath on the way down and right-hand underneath on the way back. I had only one way of turning hay—left hand underneath—so I had to set backwards on the return. Then I always seemed to get the bum fork, the one with the worn prongs and a handle made out of a piece of ash which my father always kept in the loft and which although rasped down was a bit rough and knobby.

When the hay was heavy and "scrammely" (knitted together)—not nearly as bad in my time as half a generation earlier when one meadow was a water meadow—I'd hear the sergeant-major's voice of my father urging, "Shake it out well! Don't leave any holes. Get the green bits on top to dry out."

I often left the green bits lying where they were so I could keep up. As well as turning it we rowed it, cocked it and piked it with the fork and every year I got plenty of blisters and no sympathy.

The hay was a period of panic and tension. Our house became obsessed with it mainly because of my father. Normally he was a sort of ancient Greek to us in temperament—he liked to stop and talk, to philosophise, to drag out a job until tomorrow. But during the hay he reverted to being a barbarian.

Freedom was curtailed. A new discipline which we never experienced for the rest of the year was imposed. We weren't allowed to betray any form of indifference—and that discipline was imposed on my mother and sisters, too.

One day while waiting at home for the weather to shake up I picked up a book to continue reading where I left off the night before. Pop had gone up to the quarry to view the Clare Hills and the Galtees to work out a weather forecast. He and our neighbour, Billy Gleeson, used to do short-range predictions quite accurately. When he came into the kitchen and saw me reading a book he said to the family in general: "Look at that bloody fella reading a book—in the middle of the hay!" and his voice rose at the bit after the dash.

"The hay is wet," I said, "and it's in the meadow, not here in the kitchen."

"That's not the point!" he growled. "You should be thinking about it."

That summed up his attitude. It was only afterwards when I grew up that I understood why.

In our small-farm economics there was nothing as important as the hay. It generated trepidation about what could happen. The worst was that it would rain for two months, the hay would rot, and in the winter we'd have nothing to feed the cows. The best was that we would get the hay up in spite of the friction and the panic and still be on speaking terms.

I am sure too that the panic about hay related to the size of the holding. The smaller the farm the more tension. The loss of one cow to a small farmer was a major blow. To a well-to-do farmer a loss or two could be sustained. The small farmer like my father or Bill Byrane, a quarter mile up the road, treated his cows with the reverence of a Hindu for his Brahmin bulls. The hay had to be the best. It was even then supplemented with cabbage leaves and turnips. In the fields, *geosadáns* were pulled and ditches kept trimmed to keep pasturage at its maximum. At the first sign of rushes clogged drains were opened and freed.

These things come back to me now because, although I'm in a different business, the same loyalty to an industry is necessary, the same pride in one's handiwork is demanded, the same meticulous attention to the important details of life and work. The same basic aim: to survive the year, and not owe anyone anything.

There was drudgery then about hay-making. When I go down to Pallas during the summer I still get the same feeling in a meadow I used to have forty years ago even though the machinery is there now to make hay-making a job for robots. It was the feeling then of being a small cog in a big machine. One had no control over breakfast, dinner or supper. It was the same sort of discipline I came across later in a monastery. The river flowed enticingly along one end of the meadow but we were not allowed to flirt with it until the hay was finished. I have the impression that, every year, the hay dragged on and on and on.

When Mick or Tom Toby or Paddy Hayes Coran or Jack Hanly or Jim English came to cut our hay it was a big day. My father would have the meadow opened around the gap with a scythe. He would sharpen the triangular blades of the mowing machine and delegate us to turn the backswart and rake back the few yards of freshly-mown hay at the point so that it wouldn't get caught in the teeth of the mower on the turn.

In our area the mowing machines were either Bamford or Pierce. Each had its own sound. You'd know who was cutting hay half a mile away by the sound of them because you knew the make of machine each person had. The rest of hay-making machinery—wheelrakes, swart-turners were comparatively noiseless except for one—the kicker. Jim English, near us, had one and it created an unmerciful racket. I found out a while ago that the firm of Bamford is still in existence in Uttoxeter, England but is now less renowned for mowing machines than it is for another mechanical monster which gets in my way on narrow roads, the JCB. The B stands for Bamford. I was recently in touch with a very old storemanager who worked for Pierces of Wexford during their heyday (hay-day?) and is still working, having survived a few takeovers.

I mentioned Pierce and Bamford to him as the only brand names in Ireland. He told me there were many more and the only reason we listened to the song of those machines with that of the corncrake was because their salesmen had the wholesale trade sown up in Limerick and Tipperary. He sent me pictures and information and I'm damned if I can find them now.

My generation is likely to forget that our lifetimes spanned an agricultural revolution as radical in its own small way as the industrial revolution in England. My vision of the revolution starts with the painting of Constable's *Hay Wain* (the cart with the four stakes at each corner and the hay filled in between) and ends with the heavy tractors and trailers of the silage men of today. On a more specific note it spanned a period between the use of wooden *gabhlógs* in Ballyluddy (the neighbouring townland) as forks and the neatly packaged bales of today.

I heard my father talk about the time the *gabhlógs* were used, not in his time—more like his grandfather's time. He didn't see anything too odd about it. Hay was cut in small doses with scythes. The fields then were smaller. Compare the ordnance survey map of Brackile 1844 with today's and it is clear that there were at least four fields then where there's only one now. Billy Gleeson, our neighbour, used but forks and hand-rake to pike about three acres of hay in the '50s. He called his system "surrounding it." A circle of hay was estimated and gradually rowed with forks inwards to the centre where it piled up and was made into a hand-pike. The choice of site for the pike was most important, as it always is, even now with a reek of bales. It had to be high, dry ground. There wasn't an awful lot of that to be found in the wet, humpy meadows of Coolnapisha, Brackile and Ballyluddy. Light hand pikes were a considered choice too for Billy since coming out of Ballyluddy with a big pike on a float was a risk to man and horse. As my father used to say, "You could sink without trace in some of it."

After the *gabhlóg* came the fork, not the sabre-pointed version we have today with extrusions which hold the handle but a far more primitive piece of forked iron. It was hand-forged locally with a spike at one end to go into the handle, had two six-inch prongs about a quarter of an inch thick and was not too sharp at the points. We had one stuck in the thatch of an outhouse and, like a lot of other artifacts, it was whipped as a souvenir by some American cousins. Most likely Harry told them it was used by one of our ancestors at Vinegar Hill in 1798.

The two-prong fork was the first form of farm mechanisation and was actually considered quite dangerous. There were strict rules about its use in much the same way as there are strict rules about tractors and balers now. I remember it being drummed into me never to leave a spare fork leaning against a reek or a pike but always stick it in the ground well away from the centre of activity. I remember hearing of someone being killed over in Tipperary when he slid down off a reek and on to the handle of a fork left leaning against the hay.

There was craftsmanship and dexterity associated with the hay too. There were men who could put up edge on a scythe and men who couldn't. Before the arrival of mowing-machines you could have up to six of the men rhythmically scything their way through a meadow. And when the mowing machine arrived many old men wouldn't let it into a meadow because they said it disturbed the roots of the hay. The man who couldn't keep edge up and hadn't the blade of the scythe tackled and drawn properly was left last in the row because his stopping and starting would disturb the rhythm of the good mowers.

The scythe was kind to nature. Pheasant-chicks, corncrake-chicks, and frogs were rarely dismembered as happened with the mowing machine. Even the bees' nests could be spotted and avoided. I still have memories of my father running from angry bees and scattering hay in the air all round him with a fork to ward off their attacks. I discovered an affinity between myself and bees then. I could walk up to the nest and retrieve the honey with my hand without being stung.

Anyone who spent time in a meadow in the '40s and '50s turning and twisting hay could not help remember some of the conversations of the men as they went up one row and down another. The talk didn't interfere with the rhythm and it was always interesting. I remember being beside Connie Harding the fiddler for a whole day in Uncle Jim's meadow. While I have forgotten what he said about music and fiddling he was the first adult to share ideas about sex and women with me. I still remember some of the startling details about life in London in the '40s.

I remember arguments about men's ability with forks and came to the conclusion that there was a wide spectrum of skill in the parish ranging from Chris Ryan of Cross, who, for a lightly built man, was reputed to have an extraordinary pair of arms for forking hay, to a certain man who shall be nameless who broke the handle of a fork in every meadow he attended.

In the modern meadow there's no tipping around. You either get up on your tractor and vroom, vroom or stay at home watching telly. Tipping around for us happened in unsettled weather. A pike could be got here and there where the hay was light or a few grass cocks made to get the hay off the flat. The bank of the river could be mowed between showers. Nothing sickened me more than making cocks one day, shaking them out the next, and then having to re-make them in the evening after the cows. The picture that comes back to me is of sheltering under a bush with a fork of hay up as an umbrella and listening to men tell tales with as much fatalism as woe.

"I hear so-and-so has ten acres on the flat for a week..."

"The BBC forecast says it will pick up on Thursday..."

"If we got a few hours of sun and wind..."

It was like waiting for Godot. Even pulling butts with the risk of the odd painful innoculation from a thistle or twisting *súgáns* (the hay ropes with which the pikes were tied) were signs of movement in the direction of a finish but tipping around was the limit.

The only bright moment for me on the whole hay-making scene was when my mother and the girls would bring bacon and cabbage and new potatoes to the meadow and relieve the angst with words of sympathy and confidence, inapposite to the doom written on our faces. But the meal was fit for a king.

For refreshment during hot weather we drank cold tea instead of water.

Eventually, the hay did get finished and I didn't mind the job of topping or heading pikes because the panic was gone. It was a leisurely job. We'd cut the banks of the river and bits here and there at the headlands for topping, a parsimony that preceded us for a few generations, pull the butts again, twist an extra *súgán* and walk out the gap towards home with the forks and rake on our shoulders. Then we'd look back and my father would say, "They look tidy now. They'll last until we make the reek."

CHAPTER 7

Soul

Nicker church is painted yellow. It stands out against the hill of Knockseefinn like a lighthouse—keeping an eye on the flat half of Pallasgrean parish below. There the milestones of our lives—birth, marriage, and death—were celebrated and then documented in the parish register which goes back to 1811. For birth, read baptism; for common sense, read first confession and communion; and for puberty, confirmation.

The parish priest and his curate who had separate houses—grandiose compared with ours—supervised our performance on the virtues and commandments through confession and sermons. There were pride, covetousness, lust, anger, gluttony, envy and sloth to be monitored, particularly lust. Sometimes the men would be ashamed to confess this to our priests and would cycle the ten miles to the Benedictines in Glenstal to expunge their guilt. Not so Eddie Dwyer of the garage who went to the confession box in Nicker with some whopper, confident that he could remain anonymous by disguising his voice. When he had finished his act of contrition and was leaving the box, Fr Kinnane added: "By the way, Eddie, can you do a service on my car, tomorrow?"

I don't remember much about the priests in my early days. I never remember any of them in our house. I didn't know of anyone who had a very public and explicit faith except Matt Connell, our neighbour and a postman, and Miss Coffey my teacher up to second class. Matt went to Mass every day and said the rosary in the church after all the evening funerals.

I served Mass for a few years but was never any good at it—always going in the wrong direction. One Sunday, the canon who held me back after second Mass gave me the holy water bucket in the sacristy and signalled me to precede him back out to the sanctuary again. He never said for what. There were two women kneeling apart from one another at the altar rails and I figured the exercise had to do with one or the other. I headed for Miss Coffey who was sixty years old and a spinster. Then I heard: "Come back, you eejit!"

It was a churching ceremony.

I had great difficulty in memorising Butler's *Catechism* with the "black and white" questions. They were called black and white because the most important questions were printed in bold typeface and secondary questions in Roman typeface. I was the worst in catechism out of seventy-two pupils and was kept in after class regularly as punishment. My teacher never realised that I wasn't malingering. I had a great visual memory for things I saw and if something was illustrated on the blackboard I would never forget it, but I couldn't remember lines. I had the same problem later in memorising Shakespeare.

Sanctifying grace was a big problem for me then. People were so sure about it, yet I couldn't nail it down. It existed in me, yet I couldn't feel it and didn't even know if I had it. I thought of myself as being in some way sanctified without knowing it by all sorts of goodies that came from the sacramental table. That was so unlike the way we understood things happening to us and being good for us at home. For once, we had to deviate from our ordinary way of understanding things and either take it or leave it. We took it.

It was the beginning of a split-level approach to life for me which lasted until I was in my forties.

Sociologically we were then labelled as rural, agricultural, and Catholic which made us as a class, the butt of many a cartoon in the early *Punch*. Yet the only thing many families around us had in common in terms of personal philosophies was a thick accent and the air they breathed. Our family had little enough in common with many of the people who voted the same as us, who went to the same church and played the same games.

Many of our attitudes were at loggerheads with the perceived wisdom of the locality. My father and mother had instincts—they would have acknowledged them as residual—which resented the kind of rural dogma which dominated us, and in particular, discouraged the need to develop our natural sensitivities to people and nature.

The sensual was a bad word in rural dogma. It was associated with lewdness, self-gratification, men and women with their passions out of control. From my parents I learned that it was through the senses as well as the mind that I could feel the world and be able to evaluate it and all that was in it for myself. Words of pure logic never meant a great deal to us. Abstract principles neither. The man who absentmindedly rubbed his dog behind the ears showed a rapport with the animal kingdom and had a kind of communication with it which was not expressed in philosophy or theology books.

I was encouraged to feel a sensitivity to the bush, crag, the running river. There is a time in the month of May and early June when the grass is new and shiny and dark green. I've often felt not only like lying down on it but lying down with it. This, according to my parents, was where sensitivity to people started—not the other way round. Yet the rural dogma had it that nature and animals had to be dominated in order to gratify some vision of ourselves as the only beings on earth destined for immortality.

Like the church, my family was for things and against things. There was very little grey in our lives. Yet lust, hate, pride, gluttony and so on never got much of a public airing, in the churchy sense, in our house. We were for nature, instinct, self-reliance, wit, and humour, ingenuity, dogs, books and traditional music. We were against boredom, risks, servility, pompousness, waste, greed, slyness, boasting, and spongers. We had no strong views about important things like money, organised religion, sex or third-level education. It seemed that the church's values as expounded by the priests were going in a similar direction to ours but on separate railway tracks. There's nothing new in that. The roots of our culture go back farther than fifth century Christianity in Ireland.

Homo sapiens (the natural man) from the butt-end of East Limerick could go through life without any experience of the supernatural and hang on to the belief that, all else failing, the experience will come to him at death when he sets out on some trip into eternity. This is faith. Some people have it, and they become *homo fidelis* (man of faith) on top of *homo sapiens*. Some people don't have it. Some pretend to themselves that they have it and carry on behind the scenes as *homo sapiens* but on Sundays and holy days become *homo fidelis*. It is quite easy to do so. Nobody can prove you are not a man of faith. Neither is there any obligation to prove you are.

I'm sure my father lived in this kind of twilight zone between God and the gods.

One day I was cutting rushes (to top the reek) with him in Hammersley's marsh. It must have been during the run up to first communion. As children, he always made us sit on his coat (which had a recognisable but comforting smell of sweat and Garryowen tobacco) if the grass was damp. I brought up the subject of the soul. I thought he might be able to identify what it was seeing that he killed pigs and had seen people die.

"One thing I'm sure of," he said, "It's not something like a spud or a pig's *bodlach*. The priests say the soul is immortal and no one can contradict them nor does anyone want to. They are educated men."

"I don't know what it is," he continued, "but I know that my soul—although it may not be as sanctified as they would like—is much freer down here in the marsh than it is up in Nicker."

He had problems with the Canon who asked him for £20 in 1933 when he was about to marry my mother. He refused and stood his ground because he didn't have £20 to spare. He disliked the way the Canon gutted the old church and its upstairs gallery and replaced it with a "monstrosity with concrete pillars" across the nave to support pseudo-gothic arches thus obscuring the altar. He hated the class-distinction which the seating in the new church copperfastened. The side-aisles were the penny aisles for the poor people. The two centre rows of the nave which was very wide were known as the sixpenny aisles and reserved for the best-off. Outside them were the two threepenny aisles where we sat, being neither rich nor poor. The penny, threepence, and sixpence entrance fees were paid on the way in.

My father fell out too with the curate who was a brother of the Archbishop—all over a bag of stale bread. The curate kept greyhounds and one of the shopkeepers in the village used to give him any of the loaves that had aged a bit on the shelves. My father met him coming out of the shop carrying a bran bag of stale bread and suggested he give the bread to such and such a family instead of to the greyhounds. I never heard any of this from him because he would never bad-mouth the Church or the priests.

My mother who had two brothers priests kept at him to keep his mouth shut. It was a source of embarrassment to her that when the names of all the people who contributed to the Christmas or Easter collections were read out at Mass, ours would be way down near the end. I remember, though, when he jumped from three shillings and sixpence to four-and-six. That put us in a slightly different category to what was known as the labouring class.

My mother tried too to get the rosary going on some kind of permanent basis in our house. It would go fine for a few days. Then as we sat with our backs to the fire, kneeling on the cement floor and resting our elbows on the chairs, someone would give someone else a pinch in the bum and there would be laughter. We had no great consistency, and would drop it especially when someone would accidentally say the "Holy Mary" instead of the "Hail Mary" or begin to imitate the loud, trumpet tones of Matt Connell.

The priests who came to our place had grown up in rural areas too—in County Tipperary and in a small part of County Limerick. With one exception in the latter years and possibly two, I don't remember any of them being men of the people. *Homo sapiens* had been well and truly knocked out of them.

I don't think they had any great choice in the matter either. The Church trained them like that and wanted it that way.

So, as much as many priests disliked it, they stayed on the fringes of people's lives. Their lives were defined for them so that they didn't have to plough, cut hay with a scythe, carry a cow to the bull or watch a child of theirs sick with pleurisy.

They were educated mainly in the rules governing their own lives as priests (canon law), and in the rules governing the lives of lay people (moral theology) and they felt they had to stay apart like judges in courtrooms. There was a real danger that if they didn't they might become like us. On the other hand, not being like us gave them an objectivity which came in useful when they were called upon to settle domestic or townland squabbles.

It was only after Vatican II that people were called People of God, and the priests had to make some attempt at being more than magic men with magic boxes. Many of them, especially on the missions, found their real vocation when faith and nature worked together instead of against one another.

One such man was Jim Keogh, a curate in Pallasgrean in the '60s and '70s.

He could do the *Sunday Times* crossword in an hour. He smoked, played cards, drank, and was a hopeless preacher. Yet he made a breakthrough to families in Pallasgrean whose lives had never been touched by the Church. His virtue was that he never had to protect himself from people by being "holy" or a member of the priestly club. He was at his best at weddings, hurling matches, and card games— wherever people were together and behaving normally.

I heard a woman say, "I want to belong to the Church he belongs to—whatever kind of Church that is!" Fr Keogh would be the first to stop his car and examine a wall you were building or a hurley you were fixing. He related to people where they were at and by doing that he became as vulnerable as Peter or Matthew. People who thrived on doctrine and strict rules for living didn't care for him but for many on the margins of religion he was a kind of saint.

CHAPTER 8

Blood

The pan was the round one my mother used for baking—about sixteen inches across and five inches high. On the day we killed our two pigs, usually in November, it was brought out and held under their throats to catch their warm blood. It always had a fistful of salt in the bottom to keep the blood from congealing. I was given the job of holding it. I was eight.

My career as a pan-holder lasted one year. I lost the privilege because my father saw the pain and horror on my face. He told me to quit. I was replaced by my younger brother who had more stomach for the job. I was obviously weak-kneed.

After the age of ten, I stayed in the kitchen, at ease with being a coward, and listened to the squeals of our pigs as they were brought to their place of execution. This was outside the pig-house door on the kitchen table, brought out for the day. Once one series of squeals had died down and the first pig was dispatched by a knife thrust in the jugular there was always the second series of squeals to come, an hour later. I found the tension of that period devastating and tried to keep myself busy so that I wouldn't be thinking of it. The men who came to help my father to hold the pigs weren't at all upset at what was going on but laughed and joked all the time. The pigs had come to us as bonhams in May and, in six months, I had become attached to them—in so far as anyone can become attached to a pig.

There was no question of doing a bunk on that day either. The fire had to be kept going full-blast to boil big black pots of water which would be poured, scalding hot, on the carcases so that the pig's hair could be scraped off easily.

I would put in an appearance after the first pig was safely dead but couldn't help wondering if the other pig, still alive, knew what was going to happen. When both pigs were dead I felt a great relief and actually enjoyed the rest of the day, particularly when my father, like a famous surgeon surrounded by interns, turned the opening of the pig into an exercise in anatomy and biology for us.

The pigs, scraped clean as a whistle, were first hung up by the tendons of their hind legs on short seven-foot ladders leaning against the wall of the cowhouse with their bellies facing outwards. He would slit them from tail to throat and as the intestines were released he would point out the liver, the heart, the bladder, the kidneys and so on, and would always emphasise that what each of us carried around inside of ourselves was much the same as what we saw coming out of the pig.

Although it is more than forty years now since I've seen a pig killed I'm sure there was little thrown away—the bowel perhaps and the sac with bile. Even the *bodlach* was kept to grease my father's strong boots. I didn't know what the *bodlach* was then and found out afterwards it was the male pig's private parts. The men used to throw it at one another and I'm wondering now if there was any significance to that. It was the only part of the pig they threw.

The pig's bladders were handed over to us in a special ceremony. We inflated them with a goose's quill and then kicked them around although they were a bit bockety like a rugby ball. When the skin of the bladder dried overnight it became as light as a balloon and therefore useless for football.

The spotlight suddenly switched from my father to my mother when the intestines—ten yards of them from each pig—were handed over to her and we watched the process of black-pudding making. The intestines were cut into two-foot lengths, turned inside out, scraped and scalded—an awful job—and were left overnight in salty water.

Every woman-of-the-house had her own recipe for the mixture that went into the intestines to make black puddings and some puddings were tastier than others. We knew because we got black pudding from all our neighbours and from even further afield because my father killed pigs for a lot of people who were friends and was recompensed in pork steak and black pudding—the choicest of the by-products.

We ate like kings during those autumn and winter days—pig-killing time in East Limerick.

My mother's recipe for the pudding mixture was the blood of the pig, of course, mixed with oatmeal, rice, chopped onions, allspice, pepper, bits of boiled fat which had been trimmed off the parts of the pork steak near the backbone, diced liver and pieces of lean which were trimmed off the ham and minced.

There was a lot of prawbing (a messy job with the hands) in filling puddings. Amateurs funnelled the mixture in but the experts used the index and middle finger of the left hand to keep the mouth of the intestine open while the right hand shovelled the stuff in. When the two-foot length of the pudding was filled—with a lot of gurgling and squeezing—that portion was tied in a circle and then twisted into a figure eight. This was then hung on a stick with a crook on it and dunked, up and down, in a pot of scalding hot water over the fire until it was considered cooked. Knowing when it was cooked was a tricky business because one had to keep pricking the pudding with a long needle to let out the air. When water began coming out of the little holes instead of blood, then it was cooked. We had a good supply of the timber crooks in the loft so that numerous puddings could be dunked and pricked at the same time.

Puddings couldn't be left continuously in the hot water because the skin would burst.

At the end of the day we would proudly survey all the

puddings laid out flat on newspapers on the parlour table. Most of them would go to our neighbours and relatives and I, being the oldest, had the job of delivering them on my mother's bicycle.

After the pig-killing we became painfully aware of how many relatives and friends we had.

The remaining puddings would be hung high on the hob or on the crane to be smoked before being eaten by ourselves, fried in the dripping which came from the same pig. The yearly supply of dripping, kept in jamjars, was produced by pot-rendering the slabs of lard (in which the kidneys were embedded). These were removed from the cold carcases before the pigs were cut up and put in the barrel.

It's the cutting up of the pig I remember the best because I had an important part to play. I was the one who weighed the pig.

For some reason or another this operation began the evening after the day on which we killed the pigs because I remember it many times finishing under candlelight. It took place in a shed we called the shop which used to be the workshop of my grand-uncle, Dan, the cooper. The barrels which we called "stans" were kept there to hold yellow meal, bran and sometimes oats, as well as the salty bacon.

My father, having sharpened his knives, would say, "Let's have a guess at what each pig will weigh."

We'd look at them both, hanging cold on their ladders with a spud in each mouth and a sixteen-inch sally, sharpened at both ends, wedged in the carcase to keep the flanks open. We knew they would be more than two hundred-weight (224 lbs) and less than three hundred-weight (336 lbs) so it was a question of settling on a figure in between. My father, naturally, would always be nearest to the correct weight although once I deliberately added up the weighed pieces wrongly to make myself the winner. I covered myself in glory and made him scratch his head in mystification until he totted them up for himself.

The sack of salt was ready, the stan was salted and cleaned, the ouncel, the pencil, called a "sayder" (cedar) by my father, and paper were on hand and the stiff carcase of the pig was on the kitchen table, again sequestered to the outside for an evening. We were ready.

Off came the head. It was weighted, flattened and put in the stan which had a layer of salt on the bottom. The legs, shoulders, ribs and ham were cut off, weighed and in they went in layer after layer of salt. With careful manoeuvring we fitted two pigs into one stan. No bone was hacked. No piece went in with "libbers" (ribbons or skeins of meat) hanging out of it. It was a clinical packaging exercise.

The bits which were trimmed off from the shoulder, flank, and ham were called "griskins." It was the measure of people's importance to you if you gave one family griskins from the shoulder and flank and gave others griskins from the ham, a bit of pork steak or a chunk of backbone.

The meat was covered in the stan and weights put on the lid. After two weeks or so the salt turned into brine and at the end of the sixth week the pieces were taken out dripping and hung up by iron S-hooks on the beam which crossed our kitchen, wall high.

Apart from a few chickens and fish or a fried egg on Friday this was our meat supply for the year. Pickling the meat was the Irish country people's way of saving their bacon in more ways than one. There were no fridges then and people didn't go as much to the butcher as they do now.

Later on in life I saw people preserve beef in America by smoking it and preserve fish in the Philippines by drying it under the sun. I thought back about how we were just as clever as they were.

It gives me heart to discover that some people here and there are still producing the odd stan of home-cured bacon despite the dire warnings about cholesterol and strokes. Admittedly, most of the pigs are now killed in abattoirs and delivered cold to their owner at a cost. But this faltering industry's greatest beneficiary is the head of York cabbage which has no peer as a vegetable when it is boiled with salty, home-cured bacon.

In my travels back to East Limerick to walk the fields and get rid of my madnesses I always consider a trip worthwhile if I come back with a wedge of "home-cured" in my bag. I'm convinced it is only waiting to be rediscovered—not for breakfast, dinner, and supper as my father ate it—but on some entrepreneur's menu offering the most authentic of Irish cuisine.

And forget about the Bordeaux. A mug of skim-milk will do.

CHAPTER 9

People

Billy Gleeson was a contemporary of my father's younger brothers and a bachelor. He was our nearest neighbour in the strictest sense of the word because neighbour, derived from the old English, means "near" (*neah*), "farmer" (*gebur*). He was much more than that though. The older I get the more of a permanent fixture he becomes in the complication of my past and I have to determine why.

My conclusion will be something like the assessment I was able to make of my own brother and sisters when we reached middle age. When we were young—even into our twenties and early thirties—we were a family with a blind familial acceptance of one another such as we had when we were children together. We knew all of one another's flaws and flashpoints, bickered, teased, laughed and supported—by instinct. There was never any real analysis of one another, just acceptance.

Then one day I found myself standing back from my brother and sisters. I didn't decide to stand back. It just happened. I looked at them as other people saw them because both I and they had finally become people. Perhaps they had become people long before that, had their own evaluations of one another and of me, and it was I who took longer to become people. Anyway, this moment of objectivity came to me and I was in my late thirties.

To me now in my middle fifties Billy Gleeson has become people, from being just a neighbour. It doesn't matter that he is dead.

For as long as I lived in our thatched house on the side of the hill in Brackile Billy came every night for a few hours. He never knocked at the door but opened it slowly and gently, clopped inside on the concrete floor in his nailed boots and then said "Besh" to the house. This was his own abbreviated form of "God Bless." When he left he prefaced his getting up by saying, "It's all very well for ye, I have to remove myself to Kilduff." While he was in our house he behaved as one of us and was treated like one of us. If he didn't appear at night it was because he was sick.

He lived with his aunt, a sister of his late father, Johnny, who worked on the railway all his life. He never called her anything but Auntie. Auntie had taken over when Billy's mother's died after the birth of Billy's younger brother

Packie who was nicknamed Spuddy. Every evening, hail rain or snow, she set out at four o'clock from their council cottage and walked the mile to visit relatives in Kilduff. Her eyesight was never very good and she walked with quick steps close to the grass margin in her black shawl and long black dress, feeling her way along the water-table in high laced boots. In the last ten years of her life when the road and the ditch were only a blur to her because of failing eyesight she still went to Kilduff at four o'clock but Billy walked there around nine to lead her home by the elbow. Billy loved his aunt. No son could ever be more dedicated to his mother.

That was one of the many reasons why my mother was very fond of Billy. His worst expletive was "Goodness me!". I never saw him angry or violent like other men. He was droll and we, as children, knew his repertoire of *sgéals* and riddles by heart. He never bothered adding any new ones to the repertoire. One year seemed to be the same as another to him as if time had stopped somewhere back along the line. He had no ambition to move out from Ballyluddy—except to Kilduff at night, to Pallas for Auntie's pension and to Mass in Oola. He went to Oola because he had a cousin there who had a shop. People said he once cycled to a Munster final in Thurles. Another time, during the '60s, he went to Dublin by train. My mother, to whom he confided all the titbits of news from Kilduff, Pallas and Oola, got a bonanza of information which lasted for months after the Dublin trip. She never realised, she said, that Dublin and its citizens could be so interesting while Billy was there and not when she herself or we, her children, went.

Billy was a most helpful neighbour—always available for the hay, killing the pigs, ringing bonhams and other rural calls. He was at every neighbour's beck and call and the thought of recompense never occurred to anybody. When, for some reason, my mother was at home alone and we were away some place with my father, Billy would visit her a few times to check if she was all right. He might only be passing up from the creamery or going to the dyke for a bucket of water but he always dropped in. We drank from the one stream which we called the dyke.

Billy was a gentleman but one that didn't wear gentleman's clothes. He had a suit, a topcoat and a pair of light boots for Sundays which lasted him for as long as I knew him. His weekday clothes were patched and re-patched by Auntie until one could not determine the original fabric. Yet, they were never dirty. When Auntie couldn't thread a needle Billy threaded it for her. When she couldn't sew any more Billy mended his own clothes. On wet days he would wrap a sack around his shoulders to keep out the rain.

Billy couldn't be offended. His equanimity infuriated the likes of my father and another neighbour Mick Connell, who was known as the "Lamefella." One day Billy made a sudden appearance out a gap when Mick Connell, who was a cobbler, was passing by with a young pony. The pony shied and took off and all Mick had to say afterwards was: "No wonder he shied: that *glincín* (clown) and his handful of *giobals* (patches)"

We never found it odd that Billy went around patched up to his armpits. We were patched up too but not to that extent. His fire was never much more than a handful of *cipins* and the cottage was always draughty and cold. He would light a cigarette from the fire rather than waste a match and quench the cigarette maybe twice to get two more smokes out of it. He and Auntie lived, so to speak, on the "clippings of tin".

"And still had small change left," my father would add with light-hearted spite.

It aggravated the hell out of everybody to hear that Billy had £7000 in the bank in the mid-Fifties when no one around had money like that. That information didn't come from Billy, but from a reliable source. My father accused him of it but Billy only said, "Goodness me".

He had seven or eight acres down a long boreen in Ballyluddy and in my early days kept a few cows and had milk going to the creamery. The milk churn went piggy-back on another farmer's cart because Billy had neither cart nor donkey. People said that the £7000 was made up of all Billy's creamery checks since his first, added to the price he got for all the calves since Johnny died and that they lived on Auntie's old age pension since the Forties.

"Lived on the pension?" guffawed my father. "Most of that went into the bank too and they lived on the change from the tea and sugar."

In the end, when Billy was in his late sixties and Auntie was dead, he sold the land. Everyone thought he would do up the cottage, get in running water and a toilet, buy a few armchairs, put in a fireplace and make the place comfortable for his old age. The neighbours for whom he did a lot would have liked to see him spend some of his money. But he couldn't.

Billy had never learned to spend money.

Then he got sick and was in and out of the Regional Hospital in Limerick. "Wisha I'm not great," he would say. "Th'oul sthomick is at me." And there was no comfort for him because he didn't know what comfort his neighbours were talking about. He lived in a time warp and Auntie, born in the wake of the famine, had drilled him in parsimony.

"What in the name of goodness are they widening the road at Dillon's turn for?" he would ask. "Is it only to kill themselves with speed?" By the time men went to the moon Billy could only tighten his lips and wonder what was happening around him. Most of the people he grew up with had died. The drollness left him and he began to find things to complain about. Relatives housed him and cared for him until his complaining turned to paranoia. Then he went to the City Home and he never came back.

I had been away for some years and returning home after Billy's metamorphosis visited him in his hospital bed. There was an intensity in his eyes and the old equanimity had disappeared.

"Get me out of here, Jim, they're trying to kill me. They're stealing my money, you know," he cried. I found it very distressing to turn away. I tried to penetrate to the old Billy whom we all loved but couldn't. There was someone else inside there.

It was at Jimmy Carr's evening funeral in Nicker that I heard Billy was dead and that he also was being brought to the church. The crowds were thick because of Jimmy and the role he played in the Pallas GAA.

Jimmy shared the crowds with Billy, even his guard of honour of hurlers from the parish. Jimmy would have liked that.

And the Billy from his better days would have said, in surprise, "Goodness me!"

CHAPTER 10

Steam

Jim Howard was very deaf but could lip-read. He always stopped to talk to my father or mother as he wheeled his bicycle up our hill on the way to Pallas. Our house was at the side of the road, without a gate or wall. In her later years my mother became deaf too and, for some strange reason, both she and Jim could carry on an intelligible dialogue without a single miscue. Jim was one of the strongest men I ever knew and was acknowledged as the most hardworking and productive farm hand for miles around. That was the time when strength, energy and dedication counted. Jim felt out of it now with the new farm regimes of tractors and balers and cattle carried in a truck to the mart instead of being driven to fairs.

One day he stopped to talk to me at the top of the hill. He looked down over Malachy's fields toward the creamery.

"When the small creamery went," he reminisced, "community went with it."

Being in the humour for talking he leaned on the saddle of his bicycle and added:

"We now pass one another by on tarmacadamed, narrow roads glassed in by our cars. A wave of the hand replaces the words which once related one human being to another. We are not doing things together anymore like catching hares or killing pigs or making a reek."

After this *cri de coeur* we exchanged a few more remarks and then he got up on his bicycle and rode off. But he left me with one question on my mind.

Did the men and boys who once drove asses, ponies, horses and even a jennet or two to Brackile creamery over thirty years ago remember the place now with indifference or nostalgia? Did that morning trip have any other significance beyond that of a daily chore in a rural economy? Is the place just another vandalised and derelict building with memories for us as forgotten as the autumn weeds that now wither around the doors? Or is there another story?

I think there is. I think it was more than a morning chore long ago. I think most of the boys who are now men remember it with affection. There may even be an aged pony or ass somewhere that still dreams happy dreams about it.

My uncle Jim, a placid man most of the time, presided over it. He was the manager. He weighed the milk submitted each day by his eighty-seven farmer suppliers and entered the weight in pounds in his day book. There were fifty suppliers to a page, and each evening he totted up the total delivered to the creamery that day. He was the fastest man at addition I have ever seen. At the end of every month the samples of milk from each supplier over the period were tested for butter-fat by mixing them with acid and alcohol and twisting them round in a centrifuge. I used to help him write down the results for each farmer while he fiddled with water and rubber corks. The farmers were paid on the basis of average butter-fat content multiplied by volume of their milk.

Ned Houragan was the separator man. He had a red face (from being in the proximity of steam and hot water all day) and a big smile. If you started a conversation with him you couldn't get away. Many the time he followed me fifty yards on my way home—over the road to the Greenford—because he didn't want the conversation to end. He was the first man to buy trout from me when Joe Ryan taught me to tickle them or catch them by hand.

Joe's father Tom Ryan, known as Tom Katy, was the first boilerman I knew. He was one of the few people I heard my father talk a lot about and with admiration. He was droll, modest, and kind. He dropped dead beside his boiler and was succeeded by his oldest son Mikey who held the job until the creamery closed down. I probably talked more to Mikey than to anyone else in the parish because the creamery was the place to go to when one had nothing to do. When I'd return to Brackile during the first twenty years of my grown-up life the creamery was the first place I'd head for to be briefed on what happened since I was last there. It was also the place where we picked up the morning paper.

Oddly, we did not call it the creamery but the "factory." Perhaps that was because it was such a contradiction in the quiet countryside surrounding it. It was a houseful of machinery that clanked and hissed and whirred before men who had rarely witnessed any engineering more awe-inspiring than the pulper in the hayshed. It was a place of movement, of spinning wheels and belts and noise, a pacemaker in the heart of middling-to-poor land. Pipes belched smoke and steam and in a tangle carried hot and cold water, new milk, skim-milk and cream. It was presided over by a big boiler that stood roof high in a corner and carried the hottest fire a man ever saw. It was so different—a monster beside a river from which it sucked power for its engine. It was also a kind of Incredible Hulk, generous and kind, because it converted milk into money.

But that is not all—by a long chalk.

It was a community centre, a place where men met in the morning, and exchanged the news and their comments on it. There were "no-nonsense" men who exchanged civilities but made a quick turn around and were on their way home to start a day's work already pre-planned in some kind of mental Filofax.

There were the men who hung around and talked long after the skim-milk had poured into their churns. There were the "cafflers" (pranksters) and the straight-laced, the loudmouths and the taciturns, the workers and the drones—an average cross-section of rural men you'd meet anywhere from Hokkaido to Tennessee.

I remember some of the cafflers playing a trick on Paddy Molloy from Cunnagavale. While Paddy was inside with the manager discussing the sale of conacre (meadowing) the lads untackled his ass, put the shafts of the cart around one of the steel girders holding up a 12-foot high milk tank. Then they put the ass back under the cart, re-tackled him and waited for Paddy to come out. Paddy came out and said, "Hup," but the ass wouldn't move. He couldn't. Then Paddy noticed why.

"Well," he exclaimed, "Isn't he the great hoor of an ass to get himself tangled up like that!"

Tom King used to be always late bringing his milk in spite of dire warnings from the manager. This meant that the washing-up, a lengthy process, had to be delayed while he waited for Tom. This day Tom was on his "last chance" and while the manager was waiting he impatiently walked over the road past the Greenford to our hill to meet him and give out to pay. By some fluke Tom had picked this morning to come to the creamery from the other direction and while Uncle Jim was pacing the foot of the hill Tom had come and gone, aided and abetted by Mike and Ned.

Next morning, the manager, noticing he had only a one-day supply of milk, said to Tom:

"What did you do with yesterday's milk?"

"I was here yesterday," says Tom.

"You weren't."

"I was."

Then Mikey and Ned started to laugh and Uncle Jim knew he had been had.

The greatest virtue of the creamery was that it brought

men out of their houses and long boreens to talk to one another. This was good for all of us and for the women, especially. We reaped the harvest of many conversations. Not a cow fell in a dyke nor a horse went lame but the news filtered through the creamery to a hundred houses or more. The creamery was the newsroom of five parishes. And news was important—not just radio news or newspaper news but news about people we knew.

It cracked open the isolation of the long boreen and kept people in touch with reality.

Any community such as Pallasgrean had to have a centre or centres of gravity to give definition to its people. The creameries and the churches were such. The creameries were earthy places of association and dialogue and, although almost exclusively for men, scored over the churches which, although they attracted the whole population, never lent themselves to the same degree of communication.

Yet both of them made people feel they belonged to something bigger than families and were part too of a local history in which one was most unlikely to play a major role but could be remembered forever for doing something insignificant and daft.

CHAPTER 11

Knowledge

As schools went, Brackile did its job with the three R's—readin', 'ritin', and 'rithmetic. As a matter of fact, it was a bit better than most in its preparation of pupils for secondary. Miss Coffey and the master, Bill Kennedy, who was my uncle, did the educating.

How Bill achieved this teaching position out of ten acres I never quite understood. Obviously he was clever but so were a whole lot of other fellows in the parish. He was taught by distant cousins Con and Maggie Kennedy who, I used to hear people say, drove to school on an ass and cart, sitting on a board across the cripples. When Con died people said the money wasn't there to bury him. That still shocks me deeply. I've heard old and impartial people say he played a great role in our community and somehow it went unrecognised. Con's son Michael, taught a few years in Brackile and introduced hurling to the place. Two of his students—Dick Ryan and my father—won an All-Ireland hurling championship with Limerick in 1918. Michael was succeeded by Uncle Bill. My father used to say that there was pull used in Willie's (he never called him Bill) getting the job. He claimed his mother, Bill's stepmother, had friends in high places. This was probably true. My father played a bit on the fiddle and melodeon but he never blew a trumpet. Later on, if we, his children, had something to blow about he would frown on our blowing ours too.

I think the teachers Con and Maggie had as much to do with the kind of people we are now as great grandfather William. Everyone who went to be educated by them emerged with a knowledge of geography, a love of reading and a continuing curiosity for information which might fill up the loopholes in life.

Many boys and girls who finished primary education in Brackile or Nicker in the early nineteen hundreds could do algebra and calculus. And there wasn't a sizable city, lake, or river in the world that they didn't know about.

I learned this because Billy Gleeson lived beside us, and he could unravel leaving-cert trigonometry and algebra for me in 1951. He never went beyond seventh class in Brackile. Brackile school is now closed down.

If there is a difference between now and then surely it is that most of the children now are one if not two generations removed from a lifestyle in which people had to depend more on one another and on their own craft and resources. Much of the food, clothing, utensils, implements in daily used had to be improvised. By and large things were made instead of bought.

This was an element of education which never appeared in a curriculum. Yet, to me, it was the substance of any real education I look back upon.

I can't help thinking too that there was much more communal interaction before the arrival of cars, TV sets, mechanised farming and supermarkets and before the closure of the small schools and the small creameries.

People were thrown together much more, had to mix much more, relate to each other much more and agree or disagree by consensus much more. They had to. Having to get on with neighbours and relatives was necessary because there was much more economic interdependence (even to the handing on of suits and dresses) between family and family and cousin and cousin.

Nowadays because people can hack away anonymously on their own with a lot of support from the government the art of managing personal relationships well isn't as widely practised. We don't know as much about others or communicate as much with others or depend as much on others.

One of the things which intrigued me a lot when I was growing up was watching men buy and sell at a fair or indeed deal over a few calves either at home or at the calf market in Limerick.

The calf man would come from the west and park his lorry on the side of our hill. Prices were asked and offered.

No deal was ever made quickly. It was cat-and-mouse—real negotiation. Sometimes the dealer would drive away but park at the quarry and walk back to have another round of talks. I saw the same sort of bluff going on between good forty-five card-players. It had all to do with sizing up adversaries and getting as much as you could out of them fairly. It's the same kind of thing which goes on nowadays between us and the Arabs or between us and the EC. It causes me to consider where do we get the practice for it now. Is it because we've lost the art of negotiating that we depend so much on pressure groups now?

I was always hopeless at negotiation. I started out on the wrong foot about six when I bought a kid from Danny Moloney for a threepenny bit. The kid peed on everything, jumped on the kitchen table, generally screwed up the household and I was ordered to return him. To my ever-lasting shame I never got my threepenny bit back. My father never let me forget it.

There were other facets of the rural life then which taken together could be said to form a basic ingredient of good modern-day management. Hard, unrelieved work, team-work, budgets, decision making, assessment—they were all there.

You had to budget your meat for the year. Two or three pigs? How many hens? Your potatoes: a half quarter or a quarter?

The last creamery cheque came in November and what you had in the "kitty" had to last until March. Team-work was vital whether 'twas killing a pig, saving hay, or pulling a cow out of a dyke. You were your own weatherman and by and large the local signs were a lot more reliable than the radio forecasts. People made more decisions and assessments with less help then than now.

And then, of course, there were the pure gut-things to do with survival—getting by without or by improvising things you couldn't afford. The times tested the ingenuity of people in so many ways.

Take the most obvious example of ingenuity—a product far superior, cheaper, more functional than anything we have now—the thatched mud-walled house. If you were warm in winter and cool in summer half of life's battle was won. The thick mud walls and thick thatched roof of those houses were heat resistant in summer and cold resistant in winter. And the strange thing is that they cost little more than the labour. All the ingredients lay around to be put together. No builder or architect has come up with an improvement on them.

We made hurleys, *doirníns* for scythes, handles and tillies for spades, swingletrees, clamps for this and that, put *taoibhíns* on boots and tackling. There was mathematics in making a reek or pit of spuds or in putting a bottom in a bucket. There was biology in cutting up a pig, cutting *scilleáns* or pointing scollops and there was geography in everything.

Do-it-yourself didn't mean the DIY of now. Darning, mending, re-modelling hand-me-downs were crafts which called for thought and intelligence. It was a lot of hard work for providers but must also have engendered a great feeling of achievement—the kind of feeling you get when you are in control of your environment, not controlled and frightened by it.

I sat with an old man once beside a tropical river. He was starting work on a trunk of mahogany which was thirty feet long and thirty inches in diameter. All he had was an adze. It took him three months to make an out-rigger canoe out of it. Neither he nor his grandchildren will ever see social welfare of any kind and he couldn't afford three drinks in Pallas. But I envied him his pride and skill, and his happiness.

The proof of real education, therefore, seems to depend on how you handle personal relationships, how you manage what you're at, and how you improvise and adapt when the chips are down in order to survive with dignity.

These challenges were met in much more tangible form when I was growing up. I have always counted them as the most important part of my education.

By some fluke I spent twenty-two years in classrooms at the receiving end. I'm convinced that apart from the three-R years all the others have been a glorious waste of time. And when I drop into our local hostelry in Ballyluddy to quench a summer or a winter thirst with the local menfolk (none of whom would lay claim to having scaled Parnassus), I am even more convinced that most formal education—no matter how necessary it appears in order to give us doctors, vets, priests, accountants, teachers—is no match for the real stuff which gives the cutting edge to life and the only convincing reason for getting up in the morning.

CHAPTER 12

Law

I grew up surrounded by law.

There was church law, state law, school law and domestic law.

They all melted together into a community law which frightened the devil out of us once in a while and made us conform most of the time.

We were made to bend our wills to the conscience of the community in a way that is inconceivable now. At that time there was a clear and precise community conscience from which few people deviated. I'm not so sure it exists today.

This is only becoming clear to me as I observe my

children's attitudes and behaviour. They are not yet in their teens. They seem to have little fear of church, state and school law and, I have to admit, of home law too.

Since my time church law and punishment has been de-emphasised and the focus is no longer on sin and rules but on love. State law makes more headlines about human rights issues than about justice. The teacher no longer uses the rod but refers justice back to the parents or to the principal.

One gets the impression of law and justice backing back into the Garda station, into the sacristy, into the principal's office.

In the '40s it was the authority figures representing church, state, school and home who had the impact—not the law itself. They were public figures who, between them, managed the affairs of justice in the locality more by force of their personalities than by the book.

I look around me now in Lucan, Co Dublin where I live, to find modern counterparts for the authority figures who held us in check then and one thing is quite clear. The counterparts are there but they have become invisible, almost anonymous. They are no longer features of our district like Canon Ryan was or Sergeant Jim Kelleher or Master Bill Kennedy. Neither do I wield the same kind of clout at home as my father did.

I have found myself reacting against this anonymity. I get the feeling that community leadership is being exercised by AN Other.

In Brackile NS church law and state law merged becoming one hotchpotch. This was implemented by the master who was a kind of deputy-sheriff to the canon. The canon was our master's manager and had the power to hire or fire him. Of necessity, therefore, we learned more about being good Catholics than being good citizens. I never made a distinction between sin and crime. Breaking your fast before Holy Communion and breaking the insulation crocks on the telegraph poles with stones seemed to me to be one and the same in gravity.

The master had the rod—sometimes a bamboo (which was prone to disintegrate quickly), sometimes a sally. It made him the undisputed boss. The canon also had a rod—one like Aaron's which gave him a biblical right to denounce a sinner from the altar in front of his or her peers if he took it into his head. I had a healthy fear of both of them. Except for a very rare rebellion (usually by someone who was considered not to be all there) my elders were docile too.

It is easy at this distance to understand why. Brackile had only just emerged from the authoritarian days of the landlord and the gentry who had the power to send you to, or spring you from, the gallows. By the '40s the new Irish state hadn't yet adjusted itself to freedom. Authoritarianism was everywhere.

Sergeant James Kelleher was a feature of the cross of Pallas. His figure was portly, public and visible, the incarnation of the scales of justice. Apart from my father he was the strongest of the four lawmen of my young days. He was a Corkman and possessed the acknowledged shrewdness of Cork people. His intelligence network radiated from Cunningham's Bar, Grocery and Drapery to the four corners of the parish—not, mind you—from the Garda barracks.

Nobody would dream of calling it "intelligence" then. It was not reprehensible to know everyone in the parish by sight and, sooner or later, everything that went on.

His policy seemed to have been one of keeping a tight rein on a people whose greatest crimes were not having lights on their bikes at night, being involved in an odd fracas outside our dancehall, The Brook, and having ragwort rampant in their fields. He aimed at prevention rather than cure. He warned young offenders with impartiality, reported them to their parents when necessary and occasionally dispensed justice with the toe of his boot up the bums of "young pups". He seemed to be always out and about and always in conversation with someone.

He had a human side to him which tempered the edge of his authoritarianism. He could be lured in for a "small one" at the drop of a hat. He liked horse racing and often flagged down the Limerick to Tipperary bus in Pallas whenever he wanted the conductor to drop off a bet with his turf-accountant, Con Sullivan of Oola, four miles up the road.

One particular conductor got fed up with being a courier and brought back a faked docket on the return trip. It indicated that all the sergeant's horses had won and he was being credited with the winnings. Since the sergeant had no way of knowing the truth—there was no results on radio then nor a squad car to be dispatched—he repaired to Cunningham's and celebrated. When he read the proper results in the following morning's paper (he had no winner, of course), there was one awful mad sergeant seen waiting for the Limerick bus at the cross of Pallas. Not mad that a joke was played on him but mad at the thought of having spent money he hadn't earned yet. Himself and my father were never bosom pals. They were too much alike in temperament and craftiness was their common denominator.

My father's law had little kinship with church law. I never heard him preach to us about morals and I cannot recollect him ever advising us how to react to God. I think the closest he came to the Sermon on the Mount was: "Do unto others what they would do unto you and preferably before they do it to you."

Neither can I recollect him ever emphasising much about civil law to us. As a local Peace Commissioner he must have had an interest in the practical applications of it but stopped short of having an outright faith in it. I think this was because he believed no law was absolute—whether it came from God or man. Laws, for him, were something temporary to hold things in check until the *ludramawns* got their acts together.

He left the commandments to my mother and the rules about speech and table manners. She exercised her authority without tyranny and was adept at using inducements and rewards instead of threats.

The law that was closest to my father's heart sprang from a simple philosophy that there was a right way and a wrong way to do everything. The criterion wasn't the Bible, the statute books or instruction manuals but himself and his accumulated knowledge and experience. If people disagreed with the way he did something they were automatically wrong.

There was a way to drive a nail, edge a scythe, cut a branch or tackle a horse. His values came across as laws and the one time we mutinied against him we lost. He had an edict against "following the wren" on St Stephen's Day about which he never relented. It was based on a theory we could never understand—that one shouldn't even give the impression of begging money off people.

His phrases echo from the past:

"There's no room for idlers in this house."

"Hard-boiled eggs are bad for you."

"Dry your boots for tomorrow."

"Hang up your socks on the crane."

"Don't dump the leftover cabbage leaves; give them to the cows."

"Pull the *geosadáns*."

"Why can't you notice a thing which needs to be done without having to be told to do it."

"Don't go around in wet clothes."

"Don't hit the heel of the hurley off the road."

"Go out and pull the *geosadáns*."

"It's far from wallpaper and curtains we were reared."

In spite of ourselves a lot of his imperatives in regard to industry and frugality stuck with us. We carry them around with us like the ass carries the cross on his back.

It was an awful sense of duty and responsibility too which had made him a tyrant at times. When he'd forget his major role as head of the house he could be the most relaxed, congenial and humorous man you'd meet. And even extravagant.

In the end he did let go the reins to my brother and,

having done that, kept out of the way, his term as dictator ended. I believe he was glad of it.

CHAPTER 13

Images

Years ago in Brackile I knew a happiness that I cannot find now. I go back there time after time to search for it and it eludes me. I just keep thinking of the pain I get in my hip, about the 115 mile-drive back to Dublin and wonder will the car break down. I walk the fields and the bank of the river and I can't find the romance there. I keep on doing it, year after year, hoping it will come back—if only for a flash.

This happiness that I remember and the piquancy of life then are the only things that make sense out of my existence. I don't recall ever having added anything significant to life around me later. I did my duty. It was bred in me. My people were dependable. That created its own chains from which I've never been able to extricate myself.

I still keep seeing the images though.

Townvaun tumbling down past the ruins of Tuck's Mill— its white waters saying "shshsh"—and then disappearing silently under the railway.

That "shshsh" was the background music of my childhood. A crooning. The magic voice of the river which seduced us. We knew where the holes of the freshwater crabs were, the tracks of the water-rat and moorhen, the hiding places of the brown trout.

I have now grown used to streets and concrete.

Yet the images can be summoned back as easily as switching channel on television...

Danny Moloney's mother clipped his hair to the scalp in springtime and left him a fringe which arched down to his eyebrows. He was the sixth in a family of nine. My mother called him Hitler. He left school at thirteen and went to work as a farmer's boy at a salary of £26 a year. I played with him, fought with him, lived in his house and he in mine. He was much more robust than I. I saw him take a fall when his feet tripped on concealed wire as he jumped barefooted from a ditch onto the road, six feet below. He landed on his face and hands. Then he shook himself and got up. His face was a bloody mess but he played on. The Moloneys were like that. If they hadn't been they wouldn't have survived and prospered. I met him later when he returned from England to bury his mother. I wanted him to recall the past with me. He didn't want to. We had little to say to one another.

They came every year and camped beside the railway under the red bridge—a man and his wife. No horse, no caravan, no dog. They stuck a few hooped sallies in the ground, threw a sheet of light tarpaulin over them, and that was their house. He was a tinker. While he worked, she visited the houses and asked for buckets, pans, saucepans to be mended, and, as an afterthought, milk, bread, sugar and tea to keep them alive. They stayed a few days and left at daybreak. They were nice people. He showed me how to put a bottom in a bucket.

I visit Celia now and then. I fidget after a few hours in her kitchen and want to climb the hill behind her house or go to the pub at the cross of Kilcommon. Celia, my sister, is next to me in our family and she inherited a farm in Foilacleara in the next parish of Doon. The farm runs from the bog on top of Knocknastanna down to the river in Croughmorka, a distance of almost one mile. It is bisected crossways by the Kilcommon to Reenavanagh road and vertically by a stream studded with waterfalls which forms the boundary between counties Tipperary and Limerick.

The man who gave the farm to Celia was Denis Ryan, the husband of my mother's sister Cis, and the nicest man I ever met. He wore a bowler hat on Sundays and at funerals.

I went with him to the fair of Kilcommon in December 1946. There was so much snow on the ground that the fields were level with the ditches. We drove ten weaning calves the four miles and he told me that men at fairs in the old days poured whiskey into their boots to keep their feet warm. When we got to Kilcommon he went into the pub, leaving me to mind the calves. I was frantic lest they should get mixed-up with the others and I wouldn't recognise them. He brought me out a glass of lemonade. It didn't do much to warm me: Kilcommon, up in the mountains, is a bleak and windswept village in the best of weather.

We didn't sell. On the journey home again with all our weanlings, I wondered if he had poured whiskey into his boots.

During the summer I went to Foilacleara for my holidays and, as a teenager, Denis let me do what I liked. His haymaking equipment was never in the best of shape and when I'd volunteer to grease up the mowing machine, sharpen its blades, put teeth in the gatherer or a shaft on the wheelrake, he made me feel I was God's gift to Foilacleara.

That was in sharp contrast to my image of myself in Brackile where I seemed to be able to do nothing right. That was why my brother Harry and I escaped from my father's jurisdiction so often and headed off to the marsh with our dog Buddy.

All the dogs we ever had were called Buddy. The first Buddy was a cow-dog and we didn't have enough cows or land to justify a replacement when she died so we switched to terriers.

Unlike the terrier Buddies the first Buddy was a bitch and she attracted all the male dogs of the area when she came in heat. My father was content to let nature take its course and, as in the Jack London stories, the fittest would survive and the best dog would become the sire. My father tolerated them—all but one, that was—a wolfish grey dog owned by a man whom he didn't like. And the feeling was mutual.

I was awake one summer's morning at dawn because of a cacophony of howls, growls, and barks outside....(Buddy's time had come again.) I could hear the bed-springs creaking downstairs and knew my father couldn't sleep either. I waited, knowing his patience wouldn't last and that he would get up and do something—disperse the orchestra with a few roars maybe. I heard his bedroom door open, then the sound of the parlour-door at the other side of the kitchen and the jingle of keys as the closet-door in the parlour creaked open.

Tiptoeing down the stairs I heard the parlour-window go up, and as I peeped in, there he was, bare ass—nothing on but his Horrocks shirt—sighting down the barrel of the 0.45 Webley which rested in the crook of his left arm and aiming out the window. I knew it was at the grey dog. I thought everyone in the townland must have heard the crack of the revolver shattering the dawn silence. He blew the smoke from the barrel, then looked around and saw me.

"Get back to bed."

"Did you kill him, Daddy?"

"No, I only winged him."

"Can I see?"

"No. And say nothing about this to anyone."

The 0.45 Webley dated from his Volunteer days and was kept locked in the parlour-closet and with it a leather pouch of bullets. Eventually, one day when they were all away, I took the gun out to the fields, slipped a single bullet in the chamber under the hammer and pulled the trigger. Nothing happened. (Nothing could have happened because the cylinder revolved one notch as the trigger was pulled and the hammer had to fall on the empty chamber next to it.) I kept pulling the trigger, feeling the bullet must be a dud, and expecting the hammer to come down on it again at the count of six. It hit it at the count of five and the gun went off. I hadn't pointed it at the tree I had targeted but, carelessly, in the direction of our cows which were lying down chewing the cud.

If I had killed one of them I would have left home.

Harry and I went to the marsh because we felt we could get lost there. It was the closest to danger we could get in our townland—an expanse of high rushes and sedge, crisscrossed by deep drains. It was the home of the snipe, the curlew, the fox and the hare. Our earlier Buddies were in their element there. The hunt was on all the time. We never intended to catch anything and never did—except a hare—almost. We found him asleep in his seat among the rushes. We looked at one another in astonishment. It was the first time we had come across a hare in close-up and he was bigger than we expected. I nodded to Harry to throw himself upon the hare and grab him. He thought about it. He was the nearest. Then he leaped. Hare and Harry struggled in lightning action among the rushes. An uneven struggle: with an instinctive and desperate kick—like a kangaroo—the hare thumped him in the ear and broke free.

"He'll have nightmares after that," I said.

"So will I," says Harry, brushing fur and muck off himself.

My mother was a school teacher in Newcastle-upon-Tyne before she was ordered back to Ireland by her family at the outbreak of the Black-and-Tan trouble. While my father was courting her she said he used to call her "Lozenge." I never heard him use any affectionate term to her while I was growing up. She was just our mother—a walking, working blanket of warmth and understanding. Strangely, I cannot remember as many details about her as I do about my father even though she died fifteen years after him.

Except the times she was hurt.

Running in from the dairy with a rat trap hanging from her right hand. She had reached down into a barrel for a fist of bran and the trap's saw toothed jaws clapped shut on her fingers.

Her dumbfounded look when I brought her news of the death of her younger brother killed in a car-train crash in San Francisco. She went white and walked trance-like out to the hen house where she cried, alone.

Being bitten on the arm by our three-quarter horse who resented having to haul a heavy load of hay into the haggart for the reek. He took it out on her as she held him while my father was unloading.

A splash of lime going into her eyes as she prepared for white-washing and her cries of "I'm blind, I'm blind."

And one winter's night in the kitchen while my father was out at *cuartaíocht.*

I was about eight or nine and the youngest was three. We were noisy and bold and kept on demanding a bag of bull's-eyes she had hidden in the loft beside the chimney breast. Suddenly she was at the end of her tether. She reached for the paper bag of sweets and flung them on the concrete floor where they scattered to the four corners. Then she jumped up and down crying as if in despair. I ran and put my arms round her waist and pleaded, "Don't Mammy, don't..." Then she calmed down. I was very frightened.

My father came to bring me home from national school on his bicycle on the days I hadn't taken my coat and it rained unexpectedly at dismissal time. He would come in out of the rain and wait in the hall, and I would see his head with hat on through the glass at the top of the classroom door. Sometimes he had a bran bag wrapped around his shoulders and tied with a horse nail like some medieval Irish cloak. I was always happy to see him. He was the brother of the master and I felt no fear of school while he was there.

Each of us, in our turn, was taken on the bar of his bicycle to Limerick Junction races six miles away. He never went into the enclosure but down across the fields to stand by the regulation fence where we listened to the thunder of hooves, the shouts of jockeys and saw the silken colours fly past, the sweaty sheen of horses, the flying debris of the steeplechase. On one occasion when we went by train to the Junction from the village of New Pallas we called into Mick Mettle's pub on our return. Mick took me inside the counter and kept filling whiskey glasses of Guinness for me as quickly as I would drink them. When my father was trying to balance me on the bar of the bicycle for the last lap home, I am reported to have said, "Will we go again tomorrow, Daddy?"

CHAPTER 14

Death

As the tribal family in rural Ireland becomes the nuclear family funerals become a gauge of that drift. Stand any day outside Dean's Grange cemetery in Dublin and you will see many of the funerals with only a handful of mourners in the cortege, tight-lipped and reverent. No pubs, no hanging around, not even a guffaw. Everything very efficient and packaged as if the quicker one got rid of death the better.

In rural Ireland a healthy bit of irreverence and ineffic-iency still survive at funerals. Perhaps it is because they are the last of the country rituals where time isn't counted. And when time isn't counted genuine communication is squeezed out of people.

"I'm sorry for your trouble," may not be one of the most original statements to bridge a communication gap. But it is one heck of a serious attempt at it. As a piece of genuine communication in a fragmenting community it hits the nail on the head and whether you are one of the bereaved, a mourner, or just a sympathiser, it can bring you in from the cold and make you feel part of a group which is, for once, united and unanimous about something.

Being a part of a country funeral is much more than going to a sung mass (alas, they don't sing the *Dies Irae* any more) or standing round the graveside. It has a wider social significance when the cousins and the friends one hasn't met in a long time turn up and the men, particularly, adjourn to the pub. This must be a throwback to the wakes when there was plenty of drinks, clay pipes, and snuff.

My first funeral was something like that. Mary Crowe, who lived beside us, died blowing the fire. It was fifty years ago and I was four. It was I who discovered her and raised the alarm. She smoked a pipe and hid it behind the tea canister. Four horses carried her in the black hearse out of the narrow passageway to the road gate and up the hill to Nicker.

Everyone seemed to know what to do when there was a death in the country. Some woman washed the body and laid out the deceased in a habit. The habits were often bought years ahead and showed off to contemporaries as if this were part of one's Sunday-best clothes. Men seemed to know who would dig the grave. I've heard stories of funerals being held up because inexperienced diggers underestimated the length or width of a coffin. There was hell to pay too when a grave was dug in the wrong plot because the right one wasn't properly marked.

I had read Jessica Mitford's book *The American Way of Death*, before I attended my first American funeral in Chicago in the Sixties. Even then I was amazed at the way in which the rough edges of death were softened with music and the grave was covered with a green mat which looked like grass. There wasn't a bit of clay to be seen. I couldn't help thinking of the mound of clay with the shovels stuck in it in Ireland and the way the skull and bones of some ancestors thumped down on the lowered coffin. There was no covering up the reality of death in East Limerick then.

At my second funeral, when I was six, I learned something very important—what it feels like to be drunk. It was the evening funeral of my grandfather, Henry Lande, of Coolnamona, who had a long beard and used to tell us there was a bird's nest inside it. The quarter-cask of porter was out in the dairy and Paddy (The Baker) Cummins was in charge of it.

It was a common custom to have sherry, port, and tea for the women inside and porter for men outside. As a matter of fact, the quarter-cask frequently attracted the bogus mourner—one whose sympathies were directed more to the barrel than to the coffin—so a solid citizen had to be in charge of the tap. Someone was telling me about a wake somewhere in West Limerick where a stranger walked in and people were looking at one another and wondering if it was another scrounger looking for the free porter. He took the wind out of their sails, however. Shuffling down to the room to pay his respects he curtly announced to the assembly, "I'm a friend of the corpse."

But back to the evening funeral of my grandfather. I still can't remember whether it was my own bravado in asking for and getting whiskey-glasses of porter from Paddy Cummins or whether it was the devilment in Paddy who wanted to see what would happen if such a co-operative youngster got loaded. My mother was horrified at the condition I was in and, as my grandfather was being coffined downstairs for his last ride to the church in Doon, I was being put to bed upstairs—singing.

No so long ago in the same parish of Doon I was on the fringes of a discussion about the relative merits of house-wakes and funeral parlours and I can assure you it was much more exciting than listening to people talk about hay during bad weather.

Jim Daly said it was a terrible thing nowadays that a man couldn't be buried out of his own house, that funeral parlours had taken away an important dimension of our social life, that the great tradition of people coming to the corpse-house was a great loss.

My sister Celia, a woman who is not unfamiliar with the deaths of old people, said, what do men know about corpse-houses and if he'd listen she'd tell him. She told him non-stop for about fifteen minutes. I can only remember the highlights.

"The best thing that ever happened," she declared, "was the coming of the funeral parlour because, above all else, it gave the family the time to mourn and pray. I'll give you an example: when the man of this house and the woman of this house died here, years ago, we had wakes. What happened? We were flying around like a swarm of bees for two days."

"The room had to be papered, walls whitewashed. One common car went west and the other east to gather up all the chairs, forms, stools that they could find from the neighbours as well as teapots, jugs, spoons, knives and forks. We were trying to sort who owned which spoons for months after. We spent a fortune on porter and whiskey and sherry and what for? We hadn't time to pay respects to our own dead."

She has another story: "When Uncle Bill (a bachelor uncle with no women in the house) died, I was at his bedside. One of the first things I said to myself after the Rosary for the dead was, 'My God, look at the cut of the wallpaper.' It was peeling off. I started off papering at 2.00 am with a paste cloth in one hand and a stretch of wallpaper in the other. I finished the wall inside Bill by walking over his body on the bed five or six times. Respect, how are you! It was the women who did all the work at the wakes and it is the women now who are happiest to see the end of them."

That was that.

I've got the reputation among office mates in Dublin for being "the man who likes funerals." It came about because the few times I go home to Pallas to bury old friends I always say when I come back, "It was a great funeral." I've said this many times with no disrespect for the dead.

I don't like or dislike funerals more than others who have rural roots. I think death and wakes and funerals are thing we come to grips with as we grow older. A few years ago I was sitting out at the back of my own house in Lucan. We have a rock garden in the centre of the lawn and it suddenly dawned on me that one slab of granite about two feet high was standing up like a tombstone. To enhance it and, quite by accident, there was a tall red tulip peeping up behind it. I suggested to my wife that when my time came I should be cremated and my ashes sprinkled on the rock garden.

"Much more economical," I explained, "no messing around graveyards for you and I'd be around the place permanently." Furthermore, I'd just been talking to my friend, Johnny Condron, in Kenny's pub and he told me that plots in Lucan Cemetery are now £240 with another £100 to open them. His father had bought two graves in 1924 for ten shillings.

She suggested we'd better decide on an epitaph to be chiselled on the slab. "For instance?" I asked. She came up with one in her own Filipino language: *Dito nakahimlay ang panaginip* which means "Here the dream was able to rest."

"Very good," says I. "A little bit too much chiselling, perhaps? What do you think of: 'Here lies the greatest tulip of them all'?"

Other Titles from Poolbeg

Taisce Duan

A Treasury of Irish Poems with Translations in English

Edited by Sean McMahon and Jo O'Donoghue

A choice of poetry from both the literary and the folk tradition, dating from the early 17th century to the early 20th century. The translators include some of modern Ireland's foremost poets and scholars.

POOLBEG

Prisoners

The Civil War Letters of
Ernie O"Malley

edited by
Richard English and Cormac O'Malley

Ernie O'Malley (1897-1957) was one of the most
charismatic figures to emerge from the 1916-1923
revolution in Ireland. He was converted to Republicanism
during the 1916 Rising and remained an influential
member of the IRA during both the Anglo-Irish War and
the Civil War. *On Another Man's Wound* and *The Singing
FLame*, his autobiographical accounts of the period, are
classics.

These previously uncollected letters, written while Ernie
O'Malley was imprisoned in 1923 and 1924, illuminate
this important period in modern Irish history.

POOLBEG

So You Want to Know?

(About Sex and Growing Up)

A Handbook for Parents and Young People

by
Aidan Herron and Dominic McGinley

So You Want to Know about growing up and the "facts of life"? This book tells you frankly and in detail about the physical and emotional changes that occur during puberty and adolescence, changes that often bewilder young people. It provides cheerful, uncritical advice on:

- What you need to know about friendship, feelings, emotions, dating and the opposite sex
- How to cope with pressure from family, friends, school and the media
- What dangers today's young people face as a result of alcohol, drugs, unprotected sex
- Where you can get more information and help if you need it

POOLBEG

Lovers

by
Pádraig Standún

Fr Tom Connor is a hard working, independent priest whose parish consists of a bleak coastal village and an off-shore island. Marion Warde, his housekeeper, is a girl from his home town, a reformed drug-addict and his wife in all but name. Paddy McEvilly is a typical young islander, anxious to stay at home but unable to survive without work. The island will die unless young people can be persuaded to live there. These are only three of a gallery of memorable characters in this gripping novel of modern Irish life. When Marion becomes pregnant Fr Tom faces the prospect of all his work on behalf of his flock coming to nothing.

His own career has been turbulent up till now but, no believer in clerical celibacy and a man of strong conscience, he determines to tell his people the truth. The result is a memorable story translated by Fr Standún from his best-selling novel *Súil le Breith*.

POOLBEG

The Homesick Garden

by

Kate Cruise O'Brien

"That's the trouble with trying to get your parents to like each other. They get sentimental instead. Or edgy. By edgy I mean they start edging the conversation towards sex, they start telling you things you don't really want to know. Mum made me feel awkward. I knew there was a time before I was born but I wasn't sure I wanted to hear about it—that way. In any case I didn't really see why she should feel so grateful to Dad just because he let her have a baby. I was ... he was lucky. But there was no ... mood. She was wallowing in the ... fifteen years too late."

... watchful young narrator of *The* ... rilliant first novel of Kate Cruise

OLBEG

and Honey

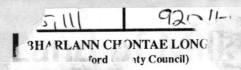

The Story of Traditional Irish
Food and Drink

by

Bríd Mahon

With an introduction
and recipes by Kathleen Watkins

When our first settlers streamed across the land bridge
from mainland Europe they found a country rich and
bountiful, flowing with milk and honey. And so it should
have remained but for the bitter accident of history. Bríd
Mahon's authoritative and mouth-watering account of
Irish foods throughout the centuries and their special
associations with wakes, weddings and the calendar
feasts of the year is a calorie-rich reminder of how sound
Ireland's worldwide reputation for prodigal hospitality is.
It also underlines how horribly wrong and avoidable the
years of famine were. Milk and honey, meat and drink,
bread and cheese—their Irish stories are told with great
readability and historical accuracy.

POOLBEG